The Somersville Bodies

The Somersville Bodies

David Osborn

Published by Dagmar Miura
Los Angeles
www.dagmarmiura.com

The Somersville Bodies

First published 2021

ISBN: 978-1-951130-67-1

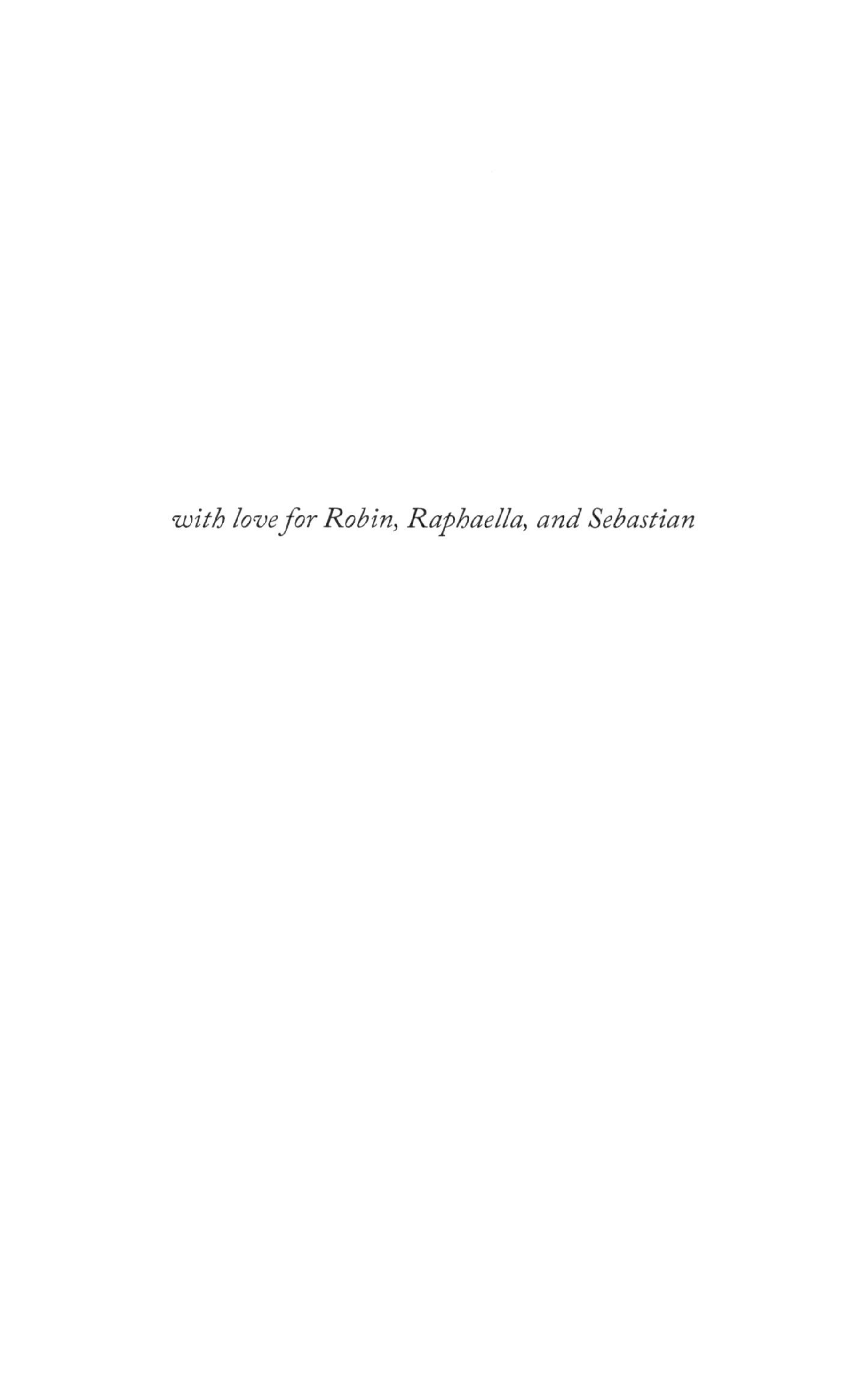

with love for Robin, Raphaella, and Sebastian

One

WHEN JANET WEISS PULLED the heavy flow-ered curtains across both second-story bedroom windows to shut out the crisp cold of a December night and then prepared for bed, she had no premonition that she was about to die.

Close by, her husband, Sidney, a gray-haired retired government cartographer, was already asleep in the queen-size bed they had occupied for the nearly forty years of their marriage. Outside their small colonial-style white-clapboarded home on the edge of one of the many narrow country roads that made up the sprawling mostly rural town of Somersville, there was the late-night quiet of win-ter settling in. Only a handful of the first responders a half mile away, the volunteer firemen, the EMT night crew and the police, were still relatively active as they changed shifts in the building and garage they occupied next to the darkened town hall and the library.

Janet felt tired but her fatigue was mostly due to excitement. It was Friday, and on Monday, she and her husband would embark for several months on a trip throughout the Middle East—Israel, Jor-dan, Egypt, and possibly Dubai—a gift to them-selves for a lifetime of hard work. Yesterday she had finally finished all the things one had to do before leaving one's home and possibly being out of touch much of the time.

She had gone to the post office to order hers and Sidney's mail held until their return; she had said good-bye to friends and neighbors and had emailed distant relatives, including a son in far-off Australia, where he represented a tech company; she had notified the electric and gas companies of her forthcoming absence until early spring, and she had fully packed hers and Sidney's principal suitcases, leaving only their two smaller carry-on bags to ready over the weekend.

Finally, she'd coped with her sister Judith Freedman's latest flap. With Sidney monopolizing the PC they shared, she had spent a busy afternoon at the library using one of three PCs that were available for library users and had texted back and forth with Judith while trying to get Judith to dismiss anxieties that she herself thought useless to pursue.

Her twin, Judith, worked nearly three hundred miles away in the state capitol building, in a second-floor carpeted executive office she shared with another, both assistants to Jason Hicks, the lieutenant governor, whose own office was reached through a wide adjoining doorway, while the governor's even larger office suite was just down the hall.

Judith, a month ago, had first cautiously, then more and more boldly, shared what she had discovered and which she insisted was possibly an incriminating exchange between Hicks and someone high up in, of all places, the West Wing of the

White House in Washington DC.

"I got onto it quite inadvertently, Janet," Judith said. "My boss mistakenly copied me on a personal email he sent. It was pure chance or accident or whatever, because he often has to copy me on important official things. And it was something I'm quite sure he never wanted me or anyone else to see."

That's how it had begun, she'd gone on. What she'd read, and although vaguely stated, had to do with the state's Orion power plant, a nuclear facility now defunct and formerly always highly controversial. It had shut down six months ago, and talking about it was seemingly normal enough. Everyone was. But why discuss it with someone in faraway Washington, of all places, where to the best of her knowledge her boss had no connections with anyone?

Her curiosity piqued, Judith was unable not to begin checking out all of Hicks's emails and texting at night and over a period of several weeks, when the Capitol building's executive suites were empty save for cleaners and herself working late.

Finding nothing further, curiosity lingered naggingly, however, especially since she was certain that what she'd accidentally been copied was something her boss would never dream of again communicating over any official computer, perhaps not even on a personal laptop at home if he had one. What he had copied her clearly indicated that he had more to say on the subject. So, why hadn't he? Why had he stopped?

And then, as her curiosity continued, she thought perhaps he hadn't stopped. Perhaps he'd gone right on but was using something different than official channels. Could that just possibly be his personal cell phone, from which he could erase whatever was communicated, and which was nearly always on his desk? So, one day while he was in a long afternoon conference with the governor just down the hall, his other assistant with him to take notes, Judith was unable to restrain herself, and her curiosity got the better of her. She got the cell phone's password from where she knew he kept all his passwords, in a small personal address book in a desk drawer.

And then during the course of a week or more when she was in the office alone and he had left his cell phone, as he often did, on his desk or in a pocket of his coat when he'd hung it up on coming to work, Judith began to read a series of texts he exchanged nearly every day with the same someone in faraway Washington. At first, the messages appeared innocent, but bit by bit a pattern emerged that Judith saw as incriminating. The two men were discussing getting rid of the shut-down Orion nuclear power station's waste somewhere within the state when doing so had created a public uproar of protests and had been voted down by the state legislature only two years ago.

Becoming frightened by what she'd learned, Judith kept it to herself for several weeks of sleepless nights before she dared even to share it with Janet, with whom she always shared everything. When she finally did, and in revealing in detail everything she'd learned, she texted, "What he's doing, Janet, is so illegal I can hardly believe it. I perhaps should blow a whistle, although I don't know to whom, and I'm sure if I did, it would be the end of my job."

Judith was always in a flap about one thing or another, and Janet was forever having to calm her down and wishing Judith had a husband to do so. But the politics and apparent illegal intrigue that were now upsetting Judith were something Janet had never had any interest in. She refused to be concerned with chicanery even if it concerned her own state and the lieutenant governor, and she stoically bore with a grain of salt Judith's emails and texting.

She responded to her sister only to make Judith happy and to calm her down, not because she cared one whit about who Lieutenant Governor Jason Hicks was scheming with in faraway Washington. *Every government is corrupt,* she thought. *So why get excited about it?* And yesterday, when saying good-bye to Judith, she'd said dismissively, "Judith, nothing has happened yet and perhaps never will."

"But Janet …"

"No buts, my dear. Save your worry for whatever day this plot, or whatever you think it is, actually happens, if ever. Meanwhile, for heaven's sake, put it to one side, keep it to yourself, and just keep doing your job that you value so much."

Finished in the bathroom and firmly closing its door to keep bedroom cold from entering it, Janet pulled back the covers on her side of the bed and picked up the book she was currently reading. Janet read a half hour every night before turning out the light, and this month the book she was reading was about a woman writer whose latest novel had been sold to a film company, and the struggle she was having to stop the movie's producer from changing what she felt were the book's most vital elements.

She had hardly settled into bed with it when she heard the knock on the front door downstairs. Startled, she struggled upright. Perhaps she'd just imagined something? Or heard a loose shutter banging? A slight night wind that had arisen? No, there it was again, and a little louder.

More curious than alarmed, Janet rose. Who on earth was it? Was some neighbor in trouble? The nearest house to hers and Sidney's was several hundred yards down the road beyond a grove of trees. Or perhaps someone's car had broken down?

Again the knock. Now quite insistent. With an exasperated sigh and a pang of jealousy glanced at her husband saved from rising by deep sleep, Janet slipped into her bathrobe, thrust her feet into slippers she always kept close to the bed, and went quickly downstairs, not turning on any lights until she had reached the front door.

"Yes?" she called out. "Who is it?"

There was no answer, but Janet wasn't in any way frightened. Somersville was virtually a crime-free town. Two years ago someone's car had been stolen, but she'd never heard of anything else, and she often wondered why they bothered to keep and pay a police force of twelve, which Sidney said was a quite normal tenth of a percent of the town's population.

When Janet took the chain off the door, unlocked and opened it, she found herself facing two middle-aged men in business suits, standing on the porch and sheltering it. One was tall and graying, the other shorter and bald. Surprised, she was staring at them, trying to remember if she'd ever seen either of them before, and if so, where, when the tall older one spoke.

"Janet Weiss?"

"Yes. I'm Janet."

"Is your husband home?"

"Yes. But he's gone to bed, I'm afraid. Who are you?"

Janet was never to find out.

Two

F AR TO THE NORTH of the state, Christmas wasn't far off, with the brilliance of fall foliage, to say nothing of lazy summer heat and vacation times, but a haunting memory. Early darkness crept in over the busy capital city, sending government workers scurrying through the accompanying cold for their cars amidst the light flakes of a first fall of snows, or for whatever public transport that would take them to the welcoming warmth and light of their homes. Everywhere there was the kind of numb thought in the mind of every worker of, "Just keep going another month. Spring will have to come someday."

One such worker, Janet Weiss's twin sister, Judith, remained at her desk, however, in the carpeted office she shared with the other assistant to the lieutenant governor. It was the end of a very long Friday during part of which she'd texted on her cell phone back and forth so much with Janet about her upsetting discovery as to make her feel nervously exhausted. Even though Janet had kept telling her, "Judith, there's always corruption in government. Don't even think of it anymore. Put it aside, and let's talk about Sidney's and my trip instead," she found it hard to let it go. Everything she'd learned kept resounding through her head and threatening to push out everything else. She had found it difficult just to look at her boss, with whom she had always had such a warm and friendly relationship, but who now appeared to her as menacing and whose every remark or request had become unwanted.

With Janet finally going off Monday, however, on her trip to Israel and Egypt and elsewhere in the Middle East and nobody with whom to share what she had learned, Judith realized that she had let important work pile up. Although tired and dying to get home to her small one-bedroom fifth-floor apartment in a complex halfway across the capital city, there to plunk down on the couch with a drink, put her feet up, and watch her favorite late-evening TV program, Judith, by nature a precise and orderly person, was determined that her desk would be relatively cleared when she came to work Monday.

Never married and with both parents sadly gone several years before, Judith had as close family only Janet, with whom she shared everything; Janet's son, Aaron, far off in Australia; and a much younger brother, Eliot, a tax accountant, who along with his wife Mary and their three children lived relatively close by in a part of the suburban belt that circled the capital and where they had bought a spacious condo on an upmarket tree-lined street relatively close to shops, including a supermarket. Tomorrow, Judith planned to take time off from her own affairs to do as she always did before Christmas.

That meant special once-a-year shopping and

coping with the crowds of pushing, elbowing people who all had the same idea and who made gift-buying more work than pleasure. There were presents to get for all of her brother's family. Eliot and Mary were easy: a new cardigan for him, new flannel pajamas for her.

The children were another story. Their widely differing ages, from five to fifteen, required thought and usually meant shopping in different places. It wasn't like Halloween when witches' and goblins' masks with hooked noses, leering awful mouths with long protruding fangs, and evil red eyes blazing hate were always a hit with kids of any age, and the more terrifying the better. Christmas meant a different kind of present for each child. A beginner's bike for the little one, perhaps; a pretty dress for the ten-year-old girl, a new skateboard for the boy.

Nothing daunted, Judith set out earnestly to clean up back work, her slim, middle-age, under-weight, and slightly bony shoulders bent forward from her office chair toward her computer monitor and the surrounding small sea of papers on her desk, her puffed-out graying hair almost obliterating any view of it. Time passed rapidly. An office wall clock, useless in an era when time was noted on computers everywhere, was mercilessly still audibly when it announced the hour—first six, then seven, then eight, and nine. And ten.

At nearly eleven and with her desk finally cleared, Judith called it a day. She shut down her computer, gratefully pushed back her office chair, rose, and went to a coat rack discreetly half-hidden by some tall filing cabinets and a coffee machine. Shrugging into a winter coat, she hoped it wouldn't be too chilly outside, for nights were indeed ever sharpening. Then, looking about as though to make sure all was right in the room, she clicked off its light and headed into the wide carpeted hall outside her office, the walls of which, between a half dozen other executive offices, were graced with ornately framed portraits of solemn former governors. Noting as she went that the lights were on in the governor's spacious suite spanning the corridor's end, Judith realized the cleaning staff were still busy and would probably be around for yet another hour.

A marble stair took her down to the building's large circular lobby, it's ceiling the high-up dome of the capitol and its embracing walls displaying busts of more of those famous in the state's history. Reaching the bottom, she nodded at the two uniformed security guards chatting at the security desk and left through an unlocked revolving door.

Outside, she paused a moment, looking down past wide-spread granite steps from the capitol to the street below and beyond it at the carefully tended park that, with its lawns and stately trees, now night-lighted, was further graced by a heroic statue of the state's founding father mounted on a massive pedestal above a fountain and surrounding pool whose waters were ever refreshed.

Evenly spaced rows of tall columned streetlamps, carefully selected for their impression of antiquity and lining the sidewalks both sides of the broad street, showed its fancifully cobbled surface deserted and its curbs bare of the usual lines of bumper-to-bumper parked cars, save for one or two belonging to other late workers.

Becoming consciously aware for the first time of the lateness of the hour, Judith turned up her collar with an injunction to herself to add a warm woolen scarf to the protection of her coat when she left home in the morning. Then, tucking her handbag under one arm and clutching a tote packed with papers and memoranda, she hastened down the steps and started on a long jaywalking diagonal toward her own car some several hundred feet away.

For the first time in a long week, Judith felt a genuine sense of relief. An agonized time of trying to know what to do had ended. She was going to follow the advice given her by Janet and do absolutely nothing about what she saw as a true scandal that she'd quite inadvertently discovered brewing between first her own state's lieutenant governor, Jason Hicks, then the someone whose name she'd gathered was Marcus-something and who worked in the White House in faraway Washington DC. Their texting had virtually spelled out a scheme for nuclear waste disposal in a defunct iron mine within the state that in the past had caused such an opposing uproar with the state's voting public.

And as though to reinforce what she had learned, there'd recently been a closed-door meeting in the governor's office down the hall that had included, besides the state's energy commissioner, Arnold Guthrie, the multibillionaire who had supported the president in the past national election and who was owner of Guthrie Associates, a giant far-reaching international construction company. Of the three other men who had attended, one was in charge of Orion, the state's now defunct nuclear power station; another was Tony Mellor, the politically powerful current head of the state legislative assembly. A fourth was four-star General Bertrand "Bomber" Berringer, in charge of all National Guard procurement.

Distraught right from the beginning about what she'd learned, Judith had become more and more so during a week of texting Janet. She was as highly moral a person as anyone, and any clearly dubious political action, especially in her own state, and particularly involving an official for whom she worked, deeply disturbed her. It made her a part, no matter how innocent, of something she felt worse than dishonest.

But now, thanks to Janet, to whom and how she would whistle-blow was no longer a burning question. Judith had always regarded Janet as being more sensible than herself, and Janet had firmly reinforced that sentiment. Any revelation of what she knew, Janet had told her, and she most certainly would be out of a job, and she had actually found herself relieved that Janet had quite firmly told her to put it all aside and forget about it.

"It's one of those cases, Judith," Janet had texted, "where you just have to be selfish and more importantly realistic. One lonely voice is not going to stop corruption which is everywhere and blowing a whistle will make you front page news, like it or not. You'd only end up destroying yourself. Eliot and Mary and the children need you like Sidney needs me. Swallow the mess in silence, my darling."

And she most certainly would, Judith had decided determinedly; and having arrived at such a decision, she felt infinitely better than she had for days.

She was halfway to her car when she suddenly became aware of the hard accelerating roar of a motor right behind her.

It was several minutes before another car driving past the capitol picked Judith out with its headlights and stopped. Its young woman driver got out, started toward her, but one look and she abruptly turned back and, barely able to speak, dialed 911.

Three

FOUR MONTHS AFTER THE unfortunate death of Judith Freedman, on her way home from work on that cold winter night, April, with its promise of spring overlaying some last vestiges of winter, had finally arrived. A bright midday sun had mostly dried up the countryside around Somersville from a recent cold rain and shone down on the town's some four thousand occupied homes, large and small. Spread out here and there, the houses of both rich and poor dotted a gently rolling pastoral landscape, marked occasionally by heavily wooded areas and small streams.

In what its citizenry called its town center, Somersville hosted close to the modern-architected and mostly glass-walled town hall and library and its voluntary first-responder units, a mini supermarket, a bank, the quick-food Lunch Pail, a pharmacy, a real estate agent, and a hardware store. All were in a semicircle around a center island of green on which there was a small bronze statue of a Minute Man, his long rifle raised defiantly.

A notably peaceful place, Somersville's excellent schools, elementary, middle, and high school, were gang free. A well-tended football field surrounded by a four-lane running track was overlooked by a small multilevel stadium that seated perhaps two hundred and which, the during the fall season, saw enthusiastic local crowds cheering on the blue uniformed Wolf Pack, the home high school team's fight against bitter rivals from other similar towns far beyond the farthest limits of sprawling Somersville.

It was Saturday, and Celeste Ellington, the town tax assessor, had decided to forgo a weekly reading group that gathered in an annex of the library in order to check out a number of residential properties for any unreported changes or additions to the principal housing. In style a typical soccer mom, she had started early, right after she'd seen her husband and two teenage sons off for the morning at the local tennis club, just beginning its first season on outdoor courts, and having finished surveying four other properties from one end of Somersville to the other, she had arrived at a fifth, 126 Northfield Road, which was relatively close to the town center.

A two story, three-bedroom classic colonial, 126 was slightly set back from a rise in the road on a property of nearly two acres. It was one Celeste had noticed from time to time when driving by in the winter, and it had been shut up since the previous December. The owners, Janet and Sidney Weiss, had gone off on a long-planned trip to the Middle East, leaving their car, a relatively expensive SUV, securely locked in a two-car garage.

Celeste saw nothing unusual in that. A number of Somersville residents often took off in the icy winter months as well as the uncertain weather in April, some to time-shares in Florida, some to Europe. She remembered Janet Weiss telling her she and her husband would be gone for at least three months, possibly even four, on a long-planned trip to the Middle East. Some few remained away past mid-May, leaving winter storm debris still scattered about, lawns uncut, shrubbery not pruned and unattended flower beds a tangled mess of wilt and brown relieved only here and there by the fresh green of newly grown weeds seeing their first light.

Such were the signs of the Weiss owners' absence. Seeing nothing wrong in that and noting there were no signs of storm damage or any break in, Celeste went around the house where a patio looked down an extensive lawn to a small stone garden shed nestled against the woods beyond.

Such sheds were often used to store a lawn-mower and heavy garden tools, or for overspill from the garage. In the past, however, the town had several times discovered some to be housing legally permitted but taxable businesses, such as creating commercial pottery for mail-order sale, or the man-ufacture of picture puzzles or wooden birdhouses.

The patio of carefully tailored and laid smooth stone had been attractively decorated with two expensive sculpted stone pots in which could be seen the dead and dried out remains of last summer's pansies and impatiens. Briefly glancing around, Celeste was at once struck by the fact that the wide patio awning, which when rolled out from above French doors to an interior living room shaded most of the patio from excessive summer sun, had never been retracted for the winter. Also striking her as odd was both patio chairs and a two-person couch seemed never to have been protectively covered, and the seats of all three were slightly marred by the winter snows on top of the autumn leaf fall.

Who on earth, Celeste wondered, would ever leave an expensive awning and patio furniture unprepared for winter, unless, perhaps and for some reason, they had departed in an excessive hurry? Not finding an answer, she left the patio and walked down the wide, slightly sloping lawn toward the shed. It was a very old building that her experience in property told her had been there long before the house was built. It perhaps dated from the late eighteenth century, when it might have actually housed someone. There were remnants of a chimney on one side.

Noticing as she went that its weather and age-worn wooden door was slightly ajar, leaving the shed's interior, like the patio awning and furniture, exposed to the winter, Celeste concluded that she was probably wasting her time. It was highly unlikely that anyone using a shed for business purposes would go away leaving it unlocked.

At the same time, it crossed her mind that perhaps the shed had been broken into. She would soon see, and she began to wonder at once how to get in touch with the couple if indeed they were conducting a business and damage or theft had occurred. Perhaps they had left a forwarding address with the post office.

Reaching the shed, she pulled the door sharply

open all the way, letting sunlight flood the shed's interior, and at the same time was unable to stifle the scream that instantly rose out of her in a sickening wave, drowning out the sound of a darkly thick cloud of flies that swarmed up at her, along with a frightened scurrying of rats.

The old shed was occupied by the ghastly grimacing, near fleshless skulls and remains of the two mostly decomposed bodies from which the flies arose.

Four

T HE YOUNG CYCLIST, NAMED Brian Cost, cursed loudly, broke his rhythm, and stopped. After reaching the crest of the rise on Northfield Road and beginning to regain the steady racing speed that he had mostly maintained over his twenty-five-mile training run, begun an hour and some minutes before, he found his way blocked by two vehicles.

One was a large oncoming commercial van that had slowed almost to a stop on the very narrow Somersville blacktopped road in order to squeeze by the other, a parked sedan directly in front of a house identified as number 126, the number painted in luminous white numbers and letters on its black roadside mailbox.

Driver's door left open, the sedan occupied the entire lane on which Brian was biking. The gap between the two vehicles was too thin to pass through for even a biker, and Brian, wearing typical racing clothes, tight gym pants and a form-fitting biker's shirt, reluctantly dismounted, took off his racing helmet, leaned his ten-speed racing bike against the back of the parked sedan, and turned to direct the oncoming van past the offending gap between the vehicles.

It was when it had gone, with a wave of thanks from the driver, and just as Brian was preparing to remount his bike and be on his way, that he heard the screams that overtook the fading sound of the receding van's motor. They seemed to come from behind the house, and they were the screams of a woman who sounded terrified.

Thoroughly startled, Brian instinctively matched the screams to whomever the driver was of the parked car blocking his lane. He leaned his bike against the car again, and when the screams were replaced with shrill cries of "Help," Brian, at once suspected a woman was being attacked, perhaps by roving coyotes or a rabid dog. Both had been reported skulking around recently, and women had been advised not to leave infants or toddlers unattended outside their homes.

Brian started for whomever was in trouble. He'd hardly got around the house when a distraught Celeste reached him, babbling incoherently about bodies and uselessly pointing down the lawn at the distant shed. Unable to get her story straight, Brian fished out his cell phone from his waist bag and thumbed in 911.

The police came, along with the town's EMT ambulance and the bright-red emergency vehicle of the town's fire chief. The decayed corpses were removed in zipped-up black body bags. The house was entered; the entire property was sealed off from the public with yellow police tape. The officer in charge of the Somersville police detectives, Detective Herman Miller, decided after a brief walkthrough of the house that the corpses were almost certainly Janet and Sidney Weiss. That no crime, in his immediate judgment, had been committed and that they were a double suicide seemed self-evident, and this was reinforced by discovery of a hypodermic syringe along with a small vial of unknown medicine on a folded pad between the two deceased.

When a suicide note was also found on the kitchen table in the house itself and next to it a nearly finished bottle of vodka and two empty glasses, DI Miller decided in agreement with Police Chief Sam Ellis against asking the state police for any assistance from a state police CSI, a crime scene investigation team of forensic experts.

The deceased couple were quickly identified from an ID bracelet on one, Miller said, and a necklace with a jeweled pendant on the other. They were indeed Sidney and Janet Weiss, who had bought and lived in the house for twenty years. Their deaths and the ghastly way they had died, their remains not to be found until so much later, were an electrifying shock to neighbors and to the many around the town who had known them.

DI Herman Miller's judgment of suicide was at once verified by the county pathologist. Dr. Alastair Crans found no evidence of any physical violence on either corpse, and upon chemical examination of the hypodermic with the vial next to it, as well as tissues from both decomposed corpses, he made the pronouncement of death by self-injection of deadly pentobarbital. Its presence, along with the half-empty bottle of vodka and the suicide note addressed to the son of the deceased and asking his forgiveness for what they had done, was deemed absolute proof of why they had died.

When the county coroner also ruled that the deaths were agreed suicides, or in legal fact possibly a murder and suicide, since one of the deceased might have administered the deadly drug to the other before injecting him- or herself, Police Chief Sam Ellis declared the case closed.

The discovery of the deceased couple immediately created, of course, the sort of unrestrained wildfire gossip and excitement that can threaten daily life in almost any small town. Residents of Somersville knotted everywhere, strangers unexpectedly becoming confidents of other strangers as well as with people with whom they were familiar.

In small disputing bunches, each and every person had a different reason for the untimely deaths. Nobody could understand why such a respected couple would kill themselves, especially on the eve of a long-planned trip abroad. A thousand motives were explored and for days little else could be heard in the town center, at the Lunch Pail, the pharmacy, or in the mini supermarket, but one theory after another.

Each explanation as to why such a couple would kill themselves was regarded by its proponent as the real one: both husband and wife had some dread terminal disease and no longer could face the final infirmities it would bring down on them; they had been involved in some sort of fraud or shady business, disclosure of which would have found them living in unbearable disgrace, even in prison; it wasn't a suicide pact—Sidney had actually murdered Janet, then subsequently in a fit of remorse, regret and fear of what disclosure of his crime would bring down on him, had taken his own life. The belief they had serious financial trouble, perhaps had been pushed to bankruptcy and ruin from investing in some Ponzi scheme, was eliminated when their wills proved them financially well off.

And above all there was the persistent question as to why they had chosen the old stone shed as a place to do themselves in. Why there? Why not in their house?

The endless speculation, gossip, and talk in Somersville eventually simmered down to an ember and found no one more relieved at the coroner's suicide verdict than portly graying Police Chief Sam Ellis. An unassuming veteran of close to forty years in law enforcement, at heart a gentle soul with no chip for anyone, Ellis felt his age. Worse, he was overcome by a kind of creeping boredom of his job in general. He was working as a police officer, he sometimes realized, when at times it seemed as though the town really had no need of any police force at all. He found himself grateful to the coroner.

"Suicide is suicide," he said to his wife, Agnes, after the coroner's verdict and when he'd left his office in the low redbrick building behind the town hall that housed his twelve-man police force and was usually fronted by five parked police cars. As he dropped wearily into his favorite sagging old easy chair in the living room of the two-bedroom home he and his wife had occupied ever since they had settled in Somersville, he said something Agnes never thought she'd hear him surrender to say since he'd taken on the job as police chief. He said, "Who cares why? It just wasn't a homicide come to burden me more than this damn job already does."

Five

O NE PERSON IN POLICE Chief Ellis's force, however, had quite a different opinion about the deaths of the Weiss couple than Chief Ellis, Detective Herman Miller, the coroner, and everybody else. This was Sergeant Cassandra Driscoll, generally known among fellow police officers as Carrie. Although she kept it to herself, she wasn't at all sure of the suicide verdict.

Almost too young to be a cop, let alone a sergeant, her slim plainclothes appearance belied both her experience and her unembarrassed dedication to her work. When on duty, she wore her natural full head of blond hair in a ponytail that stuck out of the back of a fading blue baseball cap that went with jeans and an old and worn tailored cloth jacket over a blouse or more often a T shirt lettered POLICE that hid the heavy Glock nine-millimeter handgun holstered at her hip along with her police badge, handcuffs, and cell phone.

Carrie was a relative newcomer on the Somersville police force. With it for only eight weeks, she'd come from six years with the much larger force of thirty-eight cops, six of which were detectives, at Union City, a town over three times the size of Somersville that was the hub of surrounding small-town communities, some thirty miles away. Wounded in a gun battle when she had interfered in a three-a.m. attempted 24–7 store robbery, Carrie had taken advantage of being furloughed on medical leave to be temporarily attached to the police force in Somersville, where she'd been raised and gone to school, and where she could keep an eye on her aging wheelchair-bound father, who had single-parent brought her up.

Facing a long period of inactivity and with police work compulsive in her, Carrie, however, was a dedicated cop, and taking her police work in Somersville seriously, made herself available for any job assigned. "A working rest cure," she said to anyone who asked why she was there after a laudable career in the far more important force in Union City.

The first on the suicide scene in response to bike rider Brian Cost's 911 call, Carrie had arrived in a police car, its roof lights flashing and siren slowly dying as she pulled up to a sharp stop and jumped out. She had been voluntarily filling in that day for an officer scheduled for routine highway patrol but who had reported in sick. She'd only been a half mile away when the 911 call had alerted her.

Instantly confronting Brian, who was still comforting Celeste Ellington, with a punched in "What?" and "Where?" and almost before he could get in a word, she had taken off limping slightly but like a shot for the toolshed, leaving him agape and wondering who she was and why she wasn't in uniform if driving a police car, the flashing blue and red roof lights of which she'd left on, and the car's motor still running.

Carrie had already been to number 126 and gone when Inspector Herman Miller and other police arrived, along with the EMT ambulance. But not before she had ignored the stench and the flies down at the old stone shed and had taken a good look at the decomposed deceased couple, noting the syringe on the table between them. And not before she had also checked out their car, seen through a side window in the two-car garage attached to the house where it was parked, and had silently peered through a window or two on the ground floor of the house itself to register a brief impression of both the kitchen and the living room.

Something in all of what Carrie saw didn't add up. She wasn't quite sure what—intuition based on her relatively few years' experience as police officer, or a natural ingrained refusal ever to accept any obviously lazy conclusion?

Peaceful Somersville, Carrie decided, as she drove away in the police car to resume routine road patrol along the town's labyrinth of country roads, had a double murder on its hands.

Six

Chief Ellis was soon to be burdened far more than he ever would have expected with the Weiss suicides. And the person who inadvertently would cause this was Mary Rose O'Connell, the middle-aged editor for the *Weekly Observer* in busy Union City. Located in a ground-floor office just off Main Street, its presence advertised loudly by a large lettered sign over its front door, the newspaper, with its staff of nine reporters, columnists, and subeditors, had a wide circulation not just in Union City but among the various smaller towns that surrounded it, of which Somersville was one.

The printing presses for the *Weekly Observer* were housed in a separate building once devoted to tractor repair in an outlying section of town given over to various services s such as a farm feed and grain supply company that occupied a sizeable warehouse, a garden supply company that sold lawn mowers as well as grass and flower seed and weed killer, and a lumber yard that, besides wood, sold every kind of tool used in construction.

An ardent journalist from the day she graduated state college, Mary Rose had a deep and undying loyalty not just to the *Weekly Observer* for which she had worked some thirty years, fifteen of which as editor, but to the very institution of small local newspapers. They were part of the basic fabric of American life, she often declared, decrying the fact that many were now being absorbed by larger national news syndicates, thus losing their identity, or had been forced into bankruptcy and closure from loss of sales due to television and the internet.

The daily nuts and bolts of planning an influential weekly like the Observer could often be tedious. Its twelve principal pages or so had to be filled with any and all news that would be of interest to the many local people in quite a large area around Union City who subscribed to it, and which pertained to every conceivable local event from legal or property and business matters to obituaries, wedding announcements, and coverage of high school sports.

There were extensive classified ads to be listed in a special section along with the layout of paid advertising as well as the latest in food news. Finally, and on the same page as letters to the editor, readers expected an editorial on matters that concerned them. All this, including a five-page section on the arts, had to be put to bed Thursdays so as to be available to readers Saturday morning.

Mary Rose had never had time for anything other than the *Weekly Observer*. She lived alone, in a condominium on the fringe of the town's principal golf course, eschewing a husband, a dog, or even a cat, and devoting herself twenty-four hours a day to collecting and disseminating news. To alleviate the tedium she occasionally felt, she took the liberty to spice up some events beyond the actual reporting of them. *Helps sell the paper,* she justified to herself. *Readers are always looking for excitement, even in the obits, so go for it when there was a chance that a little "yellow journalism," which wouldn't hurt anybody, might just sell more newspapers.*

Reflecting on the Weiss suicides, whose interment in Union City's Beth Israel Jewish Cemetery she planned to attend, something about the coroner's verdict of the suicide deaths in Somersville didn't seem quite right to Mary Rose. She had, several times, when covering news events herself in Somersville, bumped into Janet Weiss, once in the library, where she noted Janet as a frequent visitor, another time in the clerk's office of the town hall where they had both gone for a notarization.

Mentally scrolling back through memories of those meetings, she couldn't remember Janet as being any other than a positive-thinking happily married woman, one who put a brave face on her son working in far-off Australia, which meant her seeing him only on his rare visits home. With Sidney and herself, saving every penny for their Middle East trip, Janet had forcibly denied herself any visit to him that year.

Well, just goes to show, Mary Rose told herself when first hearing of Janet's suicide along with her husband Sidney's. *You never can tell. You think one thing about someone and they turn out just the opposite.*

More thought about it nagged, however. Had Janet actually turned out to be just the opposite? To Mary Rose's way of thinking, nobody changed much during a lifetime. What people were as kids, she'd observed, they were as adults. So, when the editor sat down in her small office, separated from the busy newsroom, to write a piece covering Janet and Sidney's deaths, she couldn't help adding a line at the end she felt would give it a little more lift and perhaps keep the story alive for another piece later. She wrote,

> Regardless of the verdict of suicide, police in Somersville are nevertheless not ruling out further investigation into the unfortunate couple's demise. Neither Somersville's Police Chief Sam Ellis, nor the detective division's Inspector Herman Miller, were available for an interview, but this paper will keep its readers informed of any new developments, regardless.

Gratuitous, she thought, *Setting a nonexistent cat among nonexistent pigeons.* That perhaps she shouldn't have, bothered her only slightly. The added bit was certain to make Chief Ellis furious. However, if that were the case, she'd weather it. Ellis, she'd found, was easy to mollify when push came to shove, and anyway, she wasn't in business to help the police; they could cope well enough with or without her. Her job was to liven up the news for the paper's readers and on the way perhaps do good not just for the *Weekly Observer* but for the cause of local newspapers everywhere from coast to coast.

Seven

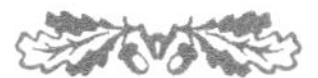

IT WAS EVENING, AND Carrie, in her own car, a beat-up eight-year-old Toyota, sadly in need of a paint job and repair to one back fender, pulled up before a low, time-worn, rough stone wall that separated the road not far from the Somersville town center from a small square house, the steep, long sloping shingled roof on one side of which marked it as having been built several hundred years previous, or even earlier. On one wall of the house, close to the front door and affixed by the town's Historical Society, a lettered wooden sign announced it had been built in 1690. Seeing it, one could only imagine that the mostly wooded area around it had once been open fields that told of it being a farm.

Inside, the house showed wide-spaced rough-hewn beams holding up the ceiling and the attic above. There were old-style hand-planed wooden tongue-in-groove walls, and the kitchen floor was of keyed-together matching flagstone. Carrie, as well as her father, had given up asking the Historical Society that owned it, and rented it to George Driscoll at a low nominal price, to modernize, but the Society had refused.

Entering the old house, Carrie unceremoniously dumped her holstered Glock handgun, cell phone, and handcuffs onto the big round kitchen table that occupied the kitchen's center and was some distance from the new gas range Carrie had scrupulously saved for and bought a year ago. Next to it was the old endlessly dented deep copper sink and the guttered oak drain board she also hoped one day to replace. Fetching two dishes and cutlery from open shelving, she dropped wearily into a chair and began to serve out pizza and pour out the wine she'd brought to her father.

A former cop himself, George Driscoll had retired early from police work after his wife's death from a long terminal illness. For years, in order to steer his daughter through her difficult teenage times in high school, then help pay her way through college, he'd worked further as a part-time relief postman, stuffing mail into the endless mailboxes that lined the labyrinth of relatively narrow blacktopped roads that made up Somersville. Now, crippled after a truck sideswiped his small regulation mail wagon adorned with its post office insignia, he lived daytimes in a wheelchair.

It was evening and Carrie had come directly to him from work before she drove back to her own permanent home in Union City and the small apartment in which, since her first rookie days, she had shared bed and board with Terry Warren, who worked in the Union City mayor's office and was a rising star in local politics.

Deeply fond of her father, aware always of how good a parent he had been, Carrie constantly worried about his frailty and having to cope on his own. Old police pals like Chief Sam Ellis, although often visitors, weren't good enough. If only there was some other woman for him beside herself. But there wasn't, and because there wasn't, she had jumped at the medical leave offer to temporarily land herself in the Somersville force. Besides keeping her busy, it gave her a far better chance at keeping an eye on her father, and she would almost always spend dinnertime with him before returning to Union City.

Daytimes, too, with the occasional chance to sneak away from police duty, enabled her to tidy up the house, to sweep and vacuum, to do his laundry, to shop and to cook the occasional meal, and above all to ease what she knew had to be the loneliness that came with his having to watch the world pass him by when he had for all his life been so much a part of it.

She and her father were still as close as they had been during all her school years, sharing the kind of closeness in which they didn't have to talk to feel each other's company. When together, there would often be long silences between them, erupting only now and then with surprising outbursts of thought, and now while he and she sipped their wine and ate pizza, George didn't speak for some time. His arthritic and often pain-tortured body was bent over an article in the Union City *Weekly Observer*, which he'd picked up that Saturday morning when a thud against the door of his cottage told him it had been delivered by Billy Yu, a local teenager. In deference to George's being wheelchair-bound,

Billy, delivering throughout Somersville from his motor scooter, would always accurately shoot the newspaper onto his doorstep rather than putting it into his roadside mailbox.

When George finally pushed away the newspaper and wheeled back slightly in his chair, he spoke in a tone that his daughter knew was deliberately mild in an effort to hold back irritation bordering on anger. George believed in news reporting that was fact and only fact. Anything else went against the grain with him. He glowered at the paper with its article, which he'd read no less than three times and had found totally offensive, and said, "One of these days someone is going to pull Mary Rose into line. Where the hell does she get off suggesting homicide?"

Carrie, Cass to him in particular, took the paper and briefly glanced at the offending article. "She doesn't actually *say* homicide, Dad."

"She insinuated it. Same damned thing. She should stick to facts."

"Maybe she thought the facts needed looking at."

"Like they hadn't been already?" But George saw an argument coming and didn't want that. Not with his daughter, anyway. It would always end up with his not being happy with her being a cop. Almost the only serious dispute they'd ever had was when she chose police work as a career. George had long protested her doing so. In his view, police work was too time-consuming for marriage and motherhood and raising children, which is why he'd quit it for postal service when he found himself a single parent.

"But police work is often fascinating, Dad," his daughter had argued. "Watching you all these years was for me like watching someone doing a picture puzzle, putting all the odd pieces together."

"When I became detective like you are now, yeah, sure, that's what I did," George said. "I put pieces together year after year while half the time taking orders from some stupid inspector who had no idea what I was talking about. And what for? Just to hear, when I presented my finished puzzle proving someone innocent, that all he wanted was a quick verdict of guilty because for him that was less work."

Even more so, her father had often gone on, police work was dangerous, as Carrie herself had only recently learned. Nailed in the foiled 24–7 store robbery gun battle six months ago, she had downed one of the two gunmen, but only after he got her first. She had earned a state commendation for bravery. "Coolest damned cop I ever saw," State Police Chief Amery Rutgers said of her performance. "Walked right through a hail of fire like it was only a light rain and kneecapped the son of a bitch right then and there from ten feet away."

She'd paid a price, however. The bullet that had torn into her thigh had lodged in bone and awaited special surgical removal, which was scheduled in two months at the big regional hospital in the state capital. Meanwhile, she walked painfully sometimes at day's end, and it was the principal reason for her transferring temporarily to the less demanding work with the Somersville police.

George silently wheeled back close to the table and seized up the newspaper again for yet another look at the offending article. He said, "Cass, who the hell did Mary Rose interview for this shit? You didn't talk to her, did you?" This time there was worry in his tone. For her to do so would have jeopardized her job.

Carrie laughed. "Me? Come off it, Dad."

Her father released a deep sigh of exasperation and, reaching for the wine bottle she'd brought with the pizza, filled his and his daughter's glasses again. As he did, and in spite of the denial, he eyed her with sudden wariness. Carrie didn't talk much; never had. She was always the mostly silent one, and you never quite knew what she was thinking. She'd stare at you with that expressionless green-gray-eyed look and you just didn't know.

She'd shown little interest in the news item, had barely glanced at it. Deliberate or not? A neighbor told him he'd seen Mary Rose coming from the Somersville police station and speaking to Carrie getting out of a police car only a day after the coroner's verdict of suicide. Had his daughter possibly talked out of turn and was covering herself, even with him?

He hated to think that she would. But you could never tell with Carrie. Her quiet, almost innocent manner, even under the most trying circumstances, disguised a streak in her character not just of skepticism about things that most other people took for granted or accepted without protest, but a stubborn defiance against any and all established attitudes. George often remembered the trying school years, times when Carrie's norm was defying teachers with "Show me" or "Prove it." Or challenged with an aggressive and demanding "Why?"

At Union City, a like attitude had often irritated Police Chief Tom Parrier, who nevertheless thought the world of her. A younger man than Chief Ellis at Somersville, and far more imaginative and open-minded, Tom was a stickler for protocol, however, and when she had constantly outsmarted him, George knew Tom had often felt forced to tolerate her endlessly wanting to know the why in every case, or her openly objecting to his reasoning only because it was the very part of her otherwise unassuming personality that had earned her detective status within four years of joining his force and over a dozen other applicants, and which now made her such a first-rate one.

Carrie brushed aside a long lock of blond hair she'd let out of its daily work ponytail and which had fallen to her shoulder. With a kind of set expression that underscored "no argument," she said, "Mary Rose could be right."

It caught George Driscoll up short. He starred at his daughter, disbelieving. "You mean that the Weiss death could be homicide?"

"Could be, Dad."

Eight

George Driscoll stared at his daughter. What on earth was she thinking? "Cass, get real." He finally said, "And probably ten times more likely that it couldn't be. Herman Miller, Chief Ellis, the county coroner—all of them have added it up to suicide."

"Herman is a fucking idiot," Carrie said, rising to put the empty pizza box in the kitchen garbage container.

"Agreed," George said. In his own opinion the man didn't have enough brains to hand out a traffic ticket, and when Carrie had taken the job as Herman's detective assistant, he'd wondered how she'd handle him. Mostly likely, he'd decided, she'd just ignore him, and he'd so far been proven right.

"And ditto Chief Ellis and the coroner," Carrie said.

George bridled at her denigration of his longtime friend Sam Ellis. "Carrie, stop it. You're talking unvarnished bullshit."

"They all passed on any serious crime investigation."

Her father's heart sank a little. *Here we go again,* he thought. *Following her own drummer for some crazy idea or another.* Everything he knew about his daughter told him that she'd now probably actually looked into Mary Rose's insinuation that there might be more than suicides with the Weiss pair, and if for no reason other than to swim against the stream. He again decided it best to change the subject and backed off, letting silence for a moment cool what he saw coming as a serious argument.

He said, "Have you talked to Terry about possibly moving back up here permanently?"

George often thought of the young political activist and budding politician who was always game to take on anything on the adverse side. He was good looking, athletic, tough, ever positive-thinking.

Struggling upward in politics, Terry had joined Carrie's father in persuading Carrie to transfer to less demanding police work at Somersville after she was injured in the shoot-out. "At least until you get the damned bullet removed, Cass," he'd said one morning. Still sleepy from making love, he'd added, "Besides, you're no use to me here, other than …" and had rolled out of bed fast and laughing to avoid her slap.

Much as Carrie would have liked to help him in his current ongoing crusade to get the town to convert what everyone called "the Old Mill" into a shopping mall and condos, she couldn't. As a police officer, she was forbidden to enter into any politics. A large nineteenth-century two-story brick structure, the Old Mill sat, forlornly abandoned, astride a rushing stream. Once employing scores in its manufacture of farm machinery and tools, its power was motivated by a huge old-fashioned paddle wheel in its interior, whose broad, slowly revolving blades, digging deep into the rushing river below, ran all the lathes, drills, heavy metal shapers, and other machinery on the mill's ground floor as well as electric light for the offices and smaller machinery on the half floor above.

"Dad, I live where Terry lives," she said to her father. "When he makes state congressman, I'll go with him to the state capital or wherever that takes him. Which could mean Washington someday. Live with it."

He said, "I wish you'd up and marry him. Why not?"

Carrie laughed. "Not ready yet, Dad." She left unspoken the words, *to hand you grandchildren to look after.*

You mean not ready to give up police work, George Driscoll thought. He suspected that a sort of anti–accepted thinking was looming in her again, the way it had over the news article. She was just like his wife in the direct unflinching gaze she would always fix on anybody when ideas adverse to theirs were jelling in her head. Never the team player, Carrie always walked her own path. And the really crazy thing about her, George thought, was that the path she walked almost always turned out to be the right one.

But police work? It still always gave him a jolt seeing her slide out of the driver's seat of a police car. "That's a cop?" he'd say to himself. But she was, all the way, and whether or not he liked it. He tossed back his wine, poured more, and gratefully grabbed up a last triangle slice of pizza from his plate before Carrie took the plate away with others to begin washing up.

Nine

RABBI SAUL GOLD REMAINED in the Beth Israel Cemetery in Union City, where for the past half hour he had stood at the very edge of the still open grave, prayer book in hand and deep in thought, a dark-suited middle-aged man whose observations of life in all its sadness during the many years he had officiated over his congregation had prematurely brought white to his hair and seamed lines to his face.

Now under the gloomy rain-threatening sky that all morning had marked the interment, and with the few mourners long departed, he remained alone, continuing to stare down at the coffin partially covered with handfuls of dirt thrown in.

There had been mostly neighbors and friends from Somersville as mourners along with a number from the congregation at temple in Union City. Interment had been first for Janet, then for Sidney. A loving couple who had come to regular worship at temple whenever they could and who had always attended at high holidays, they apparently had few relatives besides their son, who lived far away and for whom it was nigh impossible to fly to their hastily arranged funerals. There was a sister, Judith, who had died the previous year in a hit-and-run accident, he'd been told. There was a cousin or two here and there and some family he hadn't been able to contact who lived in California and whom he'd never heard either Janet or Sidney mention. The parents of both were long dead and buried only a yard of so away in the same all-Jewish cemetery.

The rabbi was filled with all the questions he always found himself asking at funerals and in cemeteries with their row after row of tombstones on which their names were inscribed along with from when to when they had lived and words that told how they had been lovingly seen by those to whom they'd been close.

The carefully raked gravel paths and the well-mown lawn between all the graves did little to hide the reality that any cemetery was filled with the bones of so many who in life had been living, breathing people, individual identities with all the laughter, the sorrow, and the hopes and dreams that were the property of every person during life.

Life was far too short for many, the rabbi thought, *and for too many an unhappy experience.* A person sprang from the utter darkness of eternity only, and in a flash, to return to it. *It wasn't fair,* he thought, *that for so many, so much of their brief moment was so despairing. God seemed strangely unforgiving at times.*

The couple he had just buried had committed suicide, he'd been told, when their death had been reported to him only a few short days ago. If so, why had they done this? Why? They'd been a mutual suicide that had occurred months ago, so that the two coffins over which he had just officiated that morning held mostly decomposed remains. They'd been found side by side in an old stone toolshed some distance from their house. Nobody had missed them. Friends and neighbors had all thought they were on a long-planned trip throughout the Middle East. What terrible sadness and pain had caused them to take their lives? What well-hidden secret? He had never once heard either complain of life, or of any illness that might have made life impossible.

Rabbi Gold was asking these questions yet another time when a voice interrupted them.

"Rabbi Gold? Rabbi?"

Startled, Rabbi Gold stepped back from the yawning grave and turned to see a pretty young blond woman confronting him with an apologetic smile. The way she was dressed, he thought at first she was one of the young college age kids from a group he counseled on religion once a month.

She said, "Please forgive me if I have disturbed you, but could I have a word?" She held up an identity card for him to see. To his surprise, it said she was Sergeant Cassandra Driscoll and a police officer.

Torn from his faraway thoughts and into an unexpected reality, Rabbi Gold for the first time saw a police car discreetly parked some distance away.

"You're police," he said, quickly trying to muster his thoughts and stating the obvious.

"Nothing serious," Carrie said. "I came to see you with a simple question about the deceased and perhaps also learn a little of their background—why you thought they had taken their own lives."

The very directness of the young woman brought the rabbi's thinking quickly alive. "Yes, yes, of course, Miss, Miss …"

"DS Driscoll. But if you'd like to keep my questioning informal, I don't mind your using my first name. It's Cassandra, although most people call me Carrie."

"I see. Of course. Thank you."

She had turned away from the grave toward the police car as though her very movement would cause him to accompany her when he noticed she was trying unsuccessfully not to limp, and apparently had one bad leg, which somehow didn't seem right for a cop. He said, "Are you all right walking? Perhaps some place we can sit down."

Carrie laughed. "It's okay. Be better when they pry the bullet loose from bone."

"Bullet?"

She didn't answer, only smiled, as though she felt she wasn't required to explain, and stared quietly back at him with a level look that said nothing. It left Rabbi Gold still trying to the absorb the sudden appearance of the young police officer, a detective, apparently, given her lack of a uniform, and her need to have questions answered about the deceased but not willing to answer any questions about herself. With another slight shock, he realized she was authentic, no question, when he finally saw the half-hidden gun and badge at her hip.

He said, "I see," and cleared his throat. "Well, okay. What was it you wanted to know?"

"First of all," Carrie said, "Affirmation about something I think I already know. The Jewish religion requires the burial of a deceased within forty-eight hours, am I right?"

"Yes. Forty-eight hours. Yes."

"But in this case, both Janet and Sidney Weiss had been dead and out of sight for over four months before interment. I'm sure you must have read the *Weekly Observer* article. It said they were found in a toolshed some distance from their house. Don't you think that as Jews intent on suicide, they would have remembered or recognized the forty-eight hours and killed themselves where they could be immediately found?"

Rabbi Gold had had the same question turning over and over in his mind ever since he had been informed of the couple's death.

Carrie said, "But they didn't seem to have. It almost seems as though they chose to die so far from their house so they wouldn't be discovered right away. Did you not possibly find that rather strange? You knew the couple."

Rabbi Gold had an immediate sense of relief that there was perhaps more than one who felt the same as he did. "I did indeed find it strange," he said. "Especially since they were quite devout. They were a very happy couple looking forward to a visit to Israel and other places in the Middle East, I believe Egypt and possibly Jordan and Dubai, they told me, and they were so devoted to the Israeli cause that they were considering perhaps someday more than a just a visit."

He paused a moment as though almost frightened to say what he thought. But when he spoke again, it was firmly assertive. "And to go one step further," he said, "I think the very idea of their suicide doesn't make sense."

Carrie said, carefully, "Does that mean you think that possibly their deaths weren't suicides?"

They had almost reached the police car, and stopped, and Rabbi Gold remained silent a rather long moment before he spoke. Then he said, "Do you mean do I think their death was possibly homicide? Yes, I do. I told that to the reporter from the *Weekly Observer* who interviewed me earlier today, and I am glad to hear the police might think so too."

When Carrie left him, she scrolled through the employees she knew at the Union City *Weekly Observer. Had to be Mary Rose O'Connell,* she thought, *the editor, or maybe Nate Wolkowski who often fills in for her.* And she remembered Mary Rose stopping her for a moment a day ago when she came out of the police station, looking for information which she'd refused to give her.

More than familiar with Mary Rose's exaggerations in print and remembering the article that had so irritated her father, Carrie wondered what sort of article she might be writing about the Weiss couple this time.

Ten

S LIGHTLY MORE THAN TWO days after Carrie met Rabbi Gold, Marcus Albright, a fleshly overweight man with a beard and the beginning of a paunch befitting his later middle years and relatively soft living, finished a mug of black coffee in the silent kitchen of his expansive home in the wealthy Bethesda outskirts of Washington DC.

It was barely six in the morning, the sun already up. Soft rays of it sifted down through the foliage of giant trees onto well-tailored lawns. The house around him was still nighttime silent and would remain so until seven, when Maria, the daily help, would arrive to begin setting the dining room table and preparing breakfast for his wife, their three daughters, and the au pair, all still asleep.

The day promised heavy heat even though summer was still around the corner. Marcus could already feel it through his impeccably laundered white shirt and cursed wearing a necktie. Folding his light summer jacket over one arm, he downed the last of his coffee and left the kitchen for the small home office where he managed all those aspects of his life that were separate from his job.

At his desk, he opened a drawer with a key from his key chain otherwise occupied with keys for the house, the garage, and a special file case at work that admitted only one other person, his assistant. From beneath several folders in the drawer, he took a letter he had placed there two days previous. Addressed to him, it had been picked up from their mailbox by his wife in one of those moments when she wasn't either on the telephone or rushing out to some committee meeting or other. Under a strict agreement that she would never open any mail addressed to him, nor he anything for her, she had placed it unopened on his desk when he had been at work.

Coming home, Marcus had closed and locked his office door before slitting the envelope open with a slender ivory letter opener he kept in a jar on his desk for pencils and extra ballpoint pens. Now, extracting and unfolding the two sheets again, he glanced casually at the first. Its printed letterhead discreetly announced that it came from Arrowsmith Ltd. An organization founded by a former Special Services officer, Andrew McClellen, Arrowsmith specialized not just in recruiting and placing mercenary soldiers in hot spots all over the world but in undercover operations the legality of most of which was highly questionable. No message or mention of services or any charge appeared on the letter's blank surface other than the capital letters FYI.

Turning to the second page, he studied it yet again, even possibly for the third time, and still with the same numb sense of shock. It was the printed PDF of a news item extracted from the *Weekly Observer,* a newspaper in a town named Union City.

Under a headline of "Possible Homicide?" the text read:

The bodies of Sidney and Janet Weiss, longtime residents of Somersville, were put to final rest yesterday at the Beth Israel Cemetery in an interment officiated over by Rabbi Saul Gold of the Beth Israel congregation in Union City. The couple, who apparently died sometime in December of last year and who were discovered at their home only this past week by Celeste Ellington, the Somersville tax assessor, were officially declared a double suicide by the Bradford County Coroner and Somersville Police Chief Sam Ellis, putting to rest wildly circulating speculation and rumor about the circumstances of their demise.

In information received from a reliable source by this newspaper, however, police are now reconsidering and investigating the possibility that the deaths were homicides.

Marcus rose, and put both the letter and its envelope into the shredder that occupied a table near his desk with a printer. He had taken a copy yesterday to the office, a relatively short distance from his own, of his immediate superior, the White House Chief of Staff, Gerald Lansdowne, a former Army four-star general whom he detested but to whom he was obliged to kowtow if he wanted to maintain the high social privilege of working in the West Wing. His much sought-after job as legal counsel and assistant to Lansdowne brought more than all its obvious perks, prestige, and money. It also had brought wide-open chances to reap in gratifyingly large unofficial rewards from lobbyists and others valuing the influence his position promised.

The whir of the shredder gone silent when it had completed its job, Marcus silently left his office and the house for a large three-car garage and his waiting BMW convertible parked between the Porsche and the family Mercedes SUV.

While on one hand Marcus cursed the early hour, on the other he welcomed the relative lack of traffic and silently thanked the stars that his home lay within the beltway that circled the nation's capital. Getting into DC, the traffic was still light. Pennsylvania Avenue was nearly devoid of vehicles as well as pedestrians and it seemed no time at all before he drew up at the heavily barred gate between the White House and the closely adjacent Executive Office Building that housed the offices and staff of the vice president along with a labyrinth of bureaucratic administrative offices.

His car, as well as himself, was recognized by the uniformed Secret Service officers on duty, but protocol was always strictly observed, and Marcus, who had rolled down his window even before he came to a stop, held out his ID card.

"Good morning."

"Good morning, sir. Hot today."

"Very." Marcus put away the ID, and when the gates swung open, drove through to find a parking slot where his license number was posted on a small plate, reserving it to him and befitting his rank. His workday had now begun.

Eleven

I T HAD TAKEN MARCUS time and many a set-back to reach his position, which his peers saw as exalted. With a Harvard law degree, he'd served two terms in Congress until voted out; he'd been a nearly victorious nominee for governor of an important state; he'd worked hard as one of the several lawyer–campaign managers of the current president, and he'd achieved prominent success as a lobbyist.

Married to another lawyer who was a tax expert with insatiable social ambitions, he rarely took time to even wonder whether she or their lifestyle were worth it. "Once on the treadmill," one of his close friends told him in one of the few moments he had ever expressed any disillusionment to anybody, "you never get off, even if allowed to."

Marcus's comfortable and well-decorated office was slightly larger than others flanking both sides of a narrow carpeted West Wing corridor and around a corner at the corridor's end from General Lansdowne's more spacious and lavishly furnished one. Reaching it, he had hardly hung his jacket over the back of his padded high-backed office chair before comfortably ensconcing himself in it, when there was a sharp rap on the door, and

Lansdowne himself appeared.

He was a tall, lantern-jawed graying man with a rigidly upright bearing that made his civilian suit look uncomfortable. Dutifully adhering to strict military hours for rising, the general was always in the office at or before seven thirty and, like Marcus, showed his patriotism with an American flag lapel pin.

Yesterday, Lansdowne had read the copy of the article Marcus had brought in and they had discussed it briefly before they had both gone to the Oval Office for their daily meeting with the president, when he came in at nine. "What do you think, Marcus?" the general had said. "Do we not discuss this with the president?"

"No, sir," Marcus had replied. "I don't think we should reveal it to him just yet," and then had added cautiously, "if at all."

To his relief, the general had agreed, visualizing as Marcus himself did that the president would have unquestionably regarded the news item as resulting from a dangerous leak. He would have lost his temper in one of his tight-lipped, barely controlled sibilant furies when words were more of a hiss than words. Voice low, barely understandable, he would have demanded to know what Lansdowne and especially he, Marcus, planned to do about it.

A hatchet-faced man close to seventy whose gray skin color matched his thinning straight back-combed hair, and whose jaws were forever slightly dark with five-o'clock shadow, the president was essentially a silent person who kept his staff and advisers too often in the dark as to his equally too often merciless thinking.

With little empathy or the quality of mercy in his makeup, but oddly and in contrast to his lavish spending habits, the president's long silences, often punctuated by his tap-tap-tapping a wooden pencil against the Resolute Desk blotter, were far more unnerving to those who served in his administration than if he had been bombastic and foulmouthed. Fear was always palpable among those confronted by the narrow-eyed silences from behind the historic Resolute Desk, but it was not fear of the moment, it was fear of what was coming when the silence was broken.

As bad if not worse for Marcus than the president's lethal silences was that Lansdowne would often clearly duck responsibility for what the president would see as a leak. That most certainly would have been the case had he seen the news item. There would have been a furious "Why hasn't Arrowsmith squelched this?" and "Who hired Arrowsmith?"

It would have done no good to even think of trying to explain to the president that he himself was the one who had suggested bringing Arrowsmith on to do whatever dirty work might be necessary to assure a wall of silence around his role in the faraway state operation that, if faulty, could seriously embarrass his presidency with evidence of corruption.

This was largely up to him, Marcus. And it meant the utmost caution where any possible necessary communication was involved with state as well as PAC officials, in spite of their intense loyalty to the president, as proved by their donations to the campaign that had given the president the White House.

On entering the Oval Office, the president's only words in response to Marcus's and General Lansdowne's respectful "Good morning, sir," were, "My briefing, Albright?"

And Marcus respectfully laid a folder on the Resolute Desk. In a state where any agreement about burying nuclear waste lay solely with a vote in the state legislature rather than, as in some states, with a popular vote, the carefully prepared folder contained extensive personal as well as political information, some damning, that he had assembled about Tony Mellor, the politically powerful head of the state legislature. It was for the president to use as leverage with which to persuade the assemblyman to sway both houses of the Legislature to go along against legislative as well as popular pressure against any multibillion-dollar action by the governor's and the president's close personal friend, Arnold Guthrie, to use a long abandoned iron mine in the state for disposal of atomic waste from the Orion nuclear power plant.

"The assemblyman," Marcus said, pointedly glancing at his watch, "is expecting your call, sir, at nine thirty."

The president glanced silently through the folder, then raising his eyes said, "A secure line?"

Lansdowne said, "Yes, sir. Both ends. I've seen to that." It meant the president could talk in absolute anonymity. His conversation with the assembly leader would neither be overheard nor recorded, and when finished, instantly erased, as though it had never existed.

A moment's silence, and the president glanced into the folder once again before saying, "You'll be advised when I am finished."

It was clearly an order. Marcus and Lansdowne silently left for the general's office, where they ran through a list of Washington figures who they could rely on to put pressure on various media to keep off the record whatever possible revelation or even suspicion they might pick up on.

Before dismissing Marcus to his own office, the general said, "Okay too for all the president's buddies and loyalists and using political pressure, but a news report like the one we've got hanging over us can explode dangerously if not killed right on the spot. This one might seem innocent at first, but as we discussed, the sooner we set up a meeting with Arrowsmith, the better. We need to make certain this sort of thing is their problem and doesn't happen again."

And Marcus had agreed.

Twelve

FOR THE UNINITIATED, ENTERING the working realm of a pathologist requires a strong stomach. There is something in the too often still air of the autopsy room that is far worse than an ordinary unpleasant smell of death and certainly so if the pathologist has two bodies out on slabs as well as the half dozen in zipped-closed plastic bags that are stored on sliding gurneys in individually separate refrigerated cells along one side of the room.

There is the sometimes pungent, sometimes acid smell of toxic chemicals and the smell unique to a lingering disease; there is the smell of body liquids, of alcohol the deceased has drunk, the stench of unleashed urine and feces; there is the smell of stale sweat and the smell of blood.

And, of course, besides this uninhibited mixture of smells, there is the sight of the death paleness of the male and female dead themselves, some young, some old, some seemingly still alive if uninjured, and all unembarrassedly naked when covering sheets have been removed.

And if an autopsy is in progress or beginning on more than one of the dead lying about on several slabs at the same time, some already opened for inspection of livers and kidneys and hearts and often all internal organs, including intestines, so that the eviscerated torso of the body resembles an open shell; others if a brain has been removed, the skull a large unoccupied bowl decorated by an inanimate nose and mouth and staring dead eyes that no one has bothered to close.

All of this was particularly true and more when Carrie Driscoll entered the county pathologist's autopsy realm to find herself enclosed by drab gray and sometimes stained walls, along with a general sense of dirt and human debris fallen to the floor along with human liquids, a sight accentuated by nakedly glaring overhead lighting.

That she was seemingly unbothered by any of it, however, when she announced who she was, was an attitude that to Dr. Alastair Crans seemed most unusual for anyone not a pathologist or even a police officer, especially a female cop who didn't look old enough to be one.

"Cold blooded little bitch," Crans muttered aloud but inaudibly. A misogynist to the core, not yet forty-five and in a profession he'd chosen as there was no responsibility in it for someone's health, the doctor had little use for women and treated their corpses with a disdain he never showed with any of the males. He took an almost unseeming delight when it came to cutting them open.

"I turned in everything necessary to the coroner," he said to Carrie, voice sour, when she ventured to say she needed some information on Janet and Sidney Weiss.

Carrie caught his tone of spite and wasn't having

it. "I'm aware of that, Dr. Crans," she said, "and equally aware that you perhaps didn't turn in everything you found."

"Shows your ignorance," the pathologist snapped back, the dismissiveness in his voice continuing. "Nothing to turn in. Bodies were too long dead to detect anything except traces of vodka. Pentobarbital disappears in fifteen days."

"No signs of violence to their arms or legs?"

"Their state of decomposition, young lady, didn't allow any such observation. And now, if you don't mind, I have a full work schedule."

Carrie ignored his already turned back. "Clothes?"

"What?"

"Their clothes, Dr. Crans. Or whatever was left of them. I'd like to see them."

This was almost the last straw with the pathologist, who spun around, his face red with anger. "Who is your superior, please?"

"Miller. Inspector Herman Miller. And then Chief Ellis."

"I know both," the pathologist said pointedly, turning his back on her again.

Carrie sighed impatiently and let him get to where he'd started to examine a corpse, some ten feet away, before she said once more, "Clothes? I need to see them. This is a homicide investigation, doctor."

Crans, spun around again and as though shot. "This is what?"

"I'm seeing the deaths of Sidney and Janet

Weiss as homicides, Dr. Crans."

Dr. Crans didn't try to hide mounting temper. His jaw moved up and down speechlessly until he snapped out. "Nonsense. It was a suicide. Neither I nor your superiors nor the coroner found evidence to indicate anything else."

"Their clothes, please. You are required by law to keep them unless or until they are claimed by relatives. And then only if their case is closed. The Weiss case is not."

It was a last straw for Dr. Crans. He didn't reply but instead shot an order to his assistant. "Show the officer the goddamned clothes," taking out his annoyance on the corpse, an elderly female, with the unnecessary violence with which he seized up a razor-sharp scalpel and slashed open her withered chest to get at her failed heart.

The assistant, a pale and vapid young man with a slight cast in one eye, a sparsely thin mustache, and the beginnings of a goatee, put down a brain he was dissecting into several thin slices with a razor-sharp scalpel and headed for a door, silently indicating to Carrie that she should follow.

An adjacent storeroom was lined with shelves containing personal items of various deceased in carefully marked boxes. Without looking at Carrie, whom he had preceded, the pathologist assistant said, "Name of the deceased?"

"There are two. Weiss, Janet and Sidney."

The assistant found the correct two boxes and took them down from the shelf where they had been stored and put them on a nearby table.

Carrie, who had slipped on surgical gloves, immediately rummaged in the few bits of clothing she found that had not rotted from the bodies' decomposition. There were a man's pajamas, both barely identifiable as such, a partial dress, and a woman's cotton underpants. It was the underpants and the man's pajamas that attracted her attention the most. She held both up, one after another, and said to the vapid assistant, "Take a look. What do you see?"

Carrie waited patiently while he obeyed silently and then finally said, "I don't see anything."

"You don't see what looks like spread-out green stains?"

He looked again and finally said, almost reluctantly, "Well, a sort of green here and there."

"And on the man's pajamas?"

A second look. "Same thing, I guess."

"Snap," Carrie said, and stuffed the remnants of both articles of clothing into a plastic bag.

Seeing her go out the door of the lab, Dr Crans reminded himself to have a word about her with Police Chief Ellis.

Thirteen

THE SOMERSVILLE POLICE STATION occupied a small redbrick building next to the fire station, with its pumper and ladder trucks, the fire chief's bright red SUV, and the EMT ambulance. The same day that found Marcus Albright coping in his stress-filled job, Police Chief Sam Ellis was in his private office. A closed door separated him from the desks and endless computer and telephone activity of his police in the low-ceilinged and somewhat cramped room beyond, and the aging law officer leaned back in his office chair, doing what his old friend George Driscoll had done. He stared unbelievingly at the *Weekly Observer.*

After a moment, he carefully and deliberately folded the newspaper and pointedly dropped it into his scrap basket before swiveling about in his chair to stare at his sergeant who stood respectfully waiting before his cluttered desk. What he'd read in the paper was something that in the chief's mind didn't fit a pattern and thus was worse than suspect. Long ago he'd learned that hunches and apparent clues jumped at too soon as positive, along with tips from so-called informers, almost never worked out.

Following patterns did. It led to successful police work, and not following them got a case nowhere except to disappointment and trouble with the police higher-ups at the state capital, who forever declared themselves embarrassed by failures among the many municipal departments they supervised.

In daily routine, any crime, whether misdemeanor or felony that dubiously passed for one, in Somersville fitted long existing, rarely troubled categories. Any police work was largely confined to traffic violations, providing protection for ongoing roadwork, keeping the curious back from fires, standing guard at the polls when voting was in progress and at schools when school was in session. The scattered papers on the chief's desk were mostly announcements or schedules of one kind or another from local organizations.

Homicide simply didn't fit into any one of Somersville's categories. Homicide just didn't exist in Somersville and never had.

"Load of bull, sergeant," he said. "I want assurance from you that you won't ever talk to any damned newspaper again, let alone the *Weekly Observer,* unless of course I authorize you to."

He shifted his gaze from Carrie to throw a brief glance at short, overweight Detective Herman Miller, who also stood nearby and who always made him think of a toad that frequented his garden at home. Miller didn't need warning, he thought. He was too dumb and lacking in initiative to have spoken to a newswoman like Mary Rose, who was notorious for revealing unauthorized police secrets. But in one way or another she had to have gotten this latest nonsense from someone on the force, and that left Driscoll's daughter, whom he wished had stayed in Union City.

When his eyes shifted back to Carrie, she said, "Chief, I didn't speak to anyone at the *Observer*."

"Then where in hell, kid, did they get this damned homicide nonsense from?"

"I don't know, sir. Possibly it came from Rabbi Gold."

"Gold? Rabbi Gold? Who the hell is he?"

"As the report says, sir. He's the rabbi who buried the couple."

"He told the paper it was a homicide?"

"I guess it was him. He certainly thought it was, and he'd met the reporter at the funeral." She added, "They were Jewish, sir."

There was a moment's intense silence during which the old chief stared at Carrie as though she were mad. He liked her. In fact, he liked her a lot; he'd liked her since she was in school and wearing braces on her teeth, and she had already proved to him what she'd proved to the police chief in Union City that on top of all that, she was a damned good cop and certainly head and shoulders better than Herman Miller, who, to his way of thinking, unfortunately outranked her.

But just the same, you had to draw a line someplace. When he finally found his voice, he said, "He thought they were a homicide because they were Jewish? Just what the hell does their religion have to do with it? They could be Muslim or Hindu for all that matters in this case."

"Sir, The Jewish religion requires burial within forty-eight hours of death."

"That's not evidence, sergeant. They arranged it that way, the Weiss couple. And they were got underground two days after they were found."

"On top of that, sir, there's clear evidence they were dragged down across the lawn to the toolshed when they were already dead."

"Evidence? What now, for God's sake?"

"Green, sir. There were definite green stains on his pajamas and on her underpants too, because if dragged, her skirt or nightgown would probably have been forced up around her torso. The green stains are clear forensic evidence, sir, that Janet Weiss and her husband were both murdered, probably in their house, and their bodies dragged across the lawn before they were left in a shed. That was done deliberately, I'm sure, so that it would be a long time, and with their bodies decomposed before being discovered, which would help eliminate clues to their murder."

Chief Ellis fought to control a rising exasperation he felt at losing control of the situation. He said, "Sergeant Driscoll, please. Forget your big-city stuff. And you may look like a first-year college girl, but you're not. You're a thirty-year-old cop and you're making something up to suit a half-cocked theory. The Weiss couple were known to be avid gardeners. If there was green on their bottoms, it more than likely came from their sitting on wet grass when weeding flower beds."

He was then silent a moment. A specter of

interference or even an investigation of his department and himself too had risen in the back of his mind. He cleared his throat and adopted a more fatherly manner, which he had found always worked with young cops. Looking down on them benignly from your years of experience usually did the trick.

He said, "Now, look here, young lady, let's get something straight. I don't mean to be hard on you, but you're new with us here in Somersville and don't quite have the hang of police work in the town yet. I understand that. So let me remind you: we don't have homicides here in Somersville. Never have had. Never will. No cause for it. People here get along with each other. Killing is someplace else, and I'm not having people disturbed with fears they have a murderer in their midst. I declared, the coroner declared, and the evidence showed, plain and simple, that the Weiss couple were a double suicide. Well, perhaps one did the other first, but that's all in their family, so to speak. Has nothing to do with the town except possibly they killed themselves because they owed back taxes or couldn't pay on their mortgage—something of that nature, and—"

"But, sir, people don't garden in their night clothes in the winter, and—"

Chief Ellis forced back instant annoyance at the interruption. He'd had enough. He said, "Case is closed, sergeant. Unless I haven't been clear enough, and don't make me have to tell you again. Work on something else. The graffiti on the middle school gym wall or whoever is using that empty up-for-sale Arnold property as a garbage dump."

Carrie glanced a last time at the *Weekly Observer* he'd thrown into his scrap basket and silently left the room.

Behind her, chief detective, Herman Miller grinned in smug satisfaction. She'd been kicked off his comfortable seniority turf for a while, at least.

Fourteen

T HE HOUSE AT 126 Northfield Road in which
Carrie thought Janet and Sidney Weiss had
unquestionably died, rather than in the stone toolshed, was in her view a pretty one. It was exactly
the kind of simple two-story clapboarded house
that she thought would suit her and Terry per-
fectly—that's if Terry would ever get around to
asking her to marry. "I'm not getting any younger,"
she'd said to him only a week ago, "and before you
know it, raising children will be more work, to say
nothing of the possible middle-aged bother of my
having them."

Terry hadn't blinked an eye. He had right away
started talking about something else, just as he
always did whenever there was mention of putting
political activism to one side and raising a family,
and with a sigh she'd resigned herself, at least for
another year, to being a cop.

Which was something you couldn't be properly, she
thought, as she stood by her parked police car, eye-
ing the house from the road, *if you gave in to the
case-closed whim of an elderly near-retiring chief like
Sam Ellis.*

There had been no serious forensic investigation in the "death house," as Carrie described it

to herself. Miller, along with Chief Ellis, had very briefly gone through the required gesture of looking for obvious signs of a struggle, but they hadn't even checked around for fingerprints. The almost instant presumption of suicide had ruled out any of that. Minds made up didn't change all so easily, and Carrie knew she'd be in serious trouble if she set one foot inside the house, perhaps even fired for insubordination, which would terribly hurt her father besides pretty much ending her police career.

But she wouldn't actually be insubordinate, she told herself, not really. She was only planning on something old Sam would do himself if he weren't so worn out, and that Herman Miller was incapable of. It was exactly what any serious investigator should be doing: looking about for any clues, no matter how few or seemingly unimportant, that might irrevocably prove homicide—in this case a double murder committed in the victims' home. Turning off the police car's motor and flashing roof lights and locking its door, she went up the short flagstone walk from the road to the front door, noticing as she went that the flowers in the beds each side of the walk had only recently been looked after and watered. The work of Celeste Ellington, she thought. It was too late to look for any possible footprints around the perimeter of the house. Winter would have erased them. There would be a FOR SALE sign up soon. It was a nice place, but would there be any buyer who wouldn't be put off by knowledge of its long dead corpses? Using the key Celeste had given her, Carrie opened up the dark-blue front door with its heavy unburnished brass lion's-head knocker and let herself in.

Celeste hadn't extended the care she'd given the outside of the house to the inside. Almost certainly, she hadn't even been in the place, Carrie thought, when she was at once enveloped by the cold, dank, dead-air smell that long shut-up houses have. And greeted by the utter silence too, a silence that was emphasized by the hands of the tall grandfather clock that had stopped at precisely twenty past four a.m., as illustrated by the painted smiling moon and the little five-pointed stars that appeared in a window just above the worn face of the old clock, whose white paint had yellowed and cracked with age.

Celeste was probably spooked, was Carrie's thought, just as she was a little herself, regardless of her police uniform and the badge and the gun at her hip. There was a sense of death everywhere. *But that's all in my imagination,* she told herself. The killers of the Weiss couple, whoever they were, would hardly be still hanging about waiting for some new victim. She was alone in the house even if she didn't feel it.

The front hall was narrow and divided by a carpeted stair leading upward. Doors led off left and right to the living room and the dining room. Someone had left gardening gloves on a hall table. *Either Janet or Sidney, but probably Janet,* Carrie thought, as they seemed small. Next to them, there was a ceramic bowl in which there were several sets of keys—household ones, one obviously car keys.

Odd, she thought. Anyone breaking into the

house could simply take the keys and drive away. Better she had taken them with her or left them with a trusted neighbor.

As she moved about the house, Carrie tried to picture what had happened that day so long ago now. Or, remembering the green stained night-clothes, surely it had been at night. Checking rooms, she saw, as DI Miller and Chief Ellis had before her, no sign of a struggle. What at first sight she did see, however, was an abundance of indications that the so-called suicides, which she now determinedly classified as murder, had occurred probably at bedtime.

There in the bedroom, her attention was drawn to the queen-sized bed the couple slept in. From the appearance of the night tables flanking it, and the pillows, two for each, Janet slept on the side closest to the windows. Bedclothes on both sides had been turned back, but quite differently. On Sidney's side, they had been nearly torn off, exposing almost all of the bottom sheet, as though he'd simply been pulled out of bed while still asleep, while Janet's were thrown back only slightly, as though she had been in bed, then had rather hastily risen.

When it came to the couple's clothes, his had all the appearance of being readied to be put on, not the look of someone planning death. They were neatly put away on a chair, his trousers and boxer shorts and undershirt folded and lying across the chair's seat, his shirt and a light windbreaker hung over the back. His shoes were paired right in front of the chair, and his socks laid across them.

Janet Weiss's clothes, hung in a closet, gave the same appearance, and oddly, curtains had been drawn as though for the night, across one of two windows looking out over the road, while curtains on the other window were half parted as though someone—Janet? Sidney?—had opened them just enough to peer down at the walk to the front door.

After noticing books half-read on both bedside tables, and where reading in each had stopped there was a book mark, Carrie imagined both Janet and Sidney in bed. Sidney had perhaps been asleep. His two pillows were flat and indented where his head would have lain. The pillows on Janet's side were still upright against the bed's headboard, and the book, her side, lay still opened. She had still been awake.

Recreating, Carrie imagined Janet rising to look out the window. But at whom? Going downstairs, had she opened the front door to someone who quickly subdued her, then rushed upstairs to tear Sidney from the bed? That possibly could have been too much of a handful for one person. So, had there perhaps been two intruders?

A last look around and Carrie suddenly realized there was something she had missed. Leaving on a trip required preparation of necessary clothes and packing them, and she saw no evidence of it. *Something's wrong there,* she thought. *Possibly their suitcases are already packed and downstairs someplace.*

She went back downstairs and first into a small room off the living room that the couple had obviously used as part office for him and part sewing room for her. In what she knew had to be Janet's corner, there was a sewing machine with an unfinished partially hemmed skirt and a worktable with a sewing box and scissors. Nothing else, and no suitcases.

On Sidney's desk there was a keyboard and a darkened PC monitor. The computer had been turned off. Without a password there was no way of getting into it to look for possible evidence. After a futile search for a password book or some other way Sidney might have had for preserving passwords, Carrie's attention was drawn to two other things.

One was a handful of pamphlets advertising holidays in both Israel and Egypt; the second comprised two sealed and fully addressed envelopes on the desk blotter. Both were stamped and awaiting to be mailed. One was to Janet's sister in the distant state capital, the other to a Christopher Weiss in Australia, who from police records she knew to be the couple's son. The addresses were handwritten. By Janet or by Sidney? The writing looked more like a woman's than a man's, and she'd seen no evidence anywhere of Janet also having a computer, neither a PC nor a laptop. Perhaps she'd used Sidney's PC.

Carrie took the letters, dropping them as evidence into a plastic bag the way she had the rotted clothing of the pair. The writing could checked by an expert Carrie knew in Union City when she'd worked there, and taking them would also avoid the possibility of Celeste or whoever mailing them when coming into the house to make it ready for sale.

In the kitchen, a tiny string of ants led her to

a mold-covered pie that had never been removed from the partially open microwave. Hit by the stench and sight of the rotting food in the refrigerator and half-choking, she slammed the fridge door shut and fled for the adjacent laundry room, where she discovered that the dryer was full of clothes and there was a tangle of now dry clothes in the washing machine.

Controlling a sudden urge to reset the tall clock in the hall and getting it ticking again, Carrie left the house, but not before picking up the key ring she'd spotted in a bowl on the hall table. As a last thought about the strange absence of any suitcases, she went direct to the garage. It had occurred to her after observing the excessive neatness of both husband and wife, as evidenced by the way they put away their clothes on retiring, that they may have finished packing and perhaps put the suitcases in their car.

On opening the garage, she was proved right. Two suitcases plus a tote bag containing sundry items were neatly stowed away in the back of the SUV parked there.

Carried locked up the garage, put the keys back where she'd found them, and went and sat on the front steps and thought. Clothes put away neatly for the night, suitcases packed and ready to go, an open book on a bedside tale, rotting food left in the microwave and the refrigerator, clothes left in the dryer and washer, stamped letters unmailed, holiday pamphlets: there was certainly proof enough that the Weiss's had not been a double suicide.

But as for homicide, nothing she saw was evidence of such. There was no blood, no visible sign of a struggle. No sign of any intrusion. Perhaps Janet had simply risen to go to the bathroom and had never pulled the curtain all the way over the window in the first place, had also never gone downstairs but had come back to bed until getting up in the morning, as had Sidney, who had thrown the bed covers all the way back on rising.

Unless the entire house was gone over again by a state police crime investigation unit, and thoroughly, with an order to look for DNA evidence that might match that of known criminals in the national crime database, she was at a dead end. Convinced, but no proof.

So what was she going to tell Sam Ellis, especially since he had firmly told her the case was closed and not to investigate further with an "or else" threat? The answer was nothing. She had proved something to herself and perhaps to the rabbi, Saul Gold, but to nobody else. She could reveal what she knew only if there was a moment when Chief Sam was in such a good fatherly mood that she dared tell him what she had been up to.

She was suddenly taken with a new thought, and with it was swept by a wave of anxiety. She had presented the chief with so much that, although possibly inconclusive, certainly pointed a serious finger. Could this possibly be the kind of case her father said he'd suffered, his presenting a pile of evidence of someone's innocence only to have it rejected because his chief found it too much work to accept it, and when just going with a guilty plea was easier?

Janet and Sidney were murdered, she was convinced of it, and they had become real to her. She felt as though she had always known them. They were ordinary decent people, innocent of any harm to anyone, and even before she'd finished searching around their house she had begun to feel a burning determination to find out who had killed them, to avenge what she more and more believed to have been their ruthless murder, to see they got the justice they deserved.

But how? What she'd just spent an hour doing should not only have been done automatically by Herman Smith but would have spiked enough curiosity in most police chiefs to have caused an order for a full-fledged investigation of homicide. Instead, she didn't dare mention what she'd been doing at the place.

After a while, she rose and went back to her police car, started it up, and drove off. She still hadn't found out who was tipping garbage onto another person's front lawn, but there was one more thing she thought she could try first for the Weiss couple that might not be evidence but could at least possibly help paint a non-suicidal picture of their last few months, and perhaps even help to convince Ellis.

Fifteen

T HE PUBLIC LIBRARY AT Somersville was set back from the Town Hall, also a low one-story modern building, by a wide stretch of green and a war memorial where a bronze plaque listing those from Somersville who had died fighting for their country was embedded in a flag-flanked huge granite boulder roughly shaped as an obelisk.

Inside, the library was a quiet well-lit place, as modern as its exterior, with a wing for children's literature and a spacious annex for lectures or meetings such as reading clubs. On entering, a front counter-like desk was a barrier to a lengthy cabinet of small file drawers an aisle distance behind it and which catalogued the several thousand books carefully arranged on a dozen rows of shelves extending the full depth of the room.

At the counter, Margaret Tate, the head librarian, a trim, fortyish, scholastic-looking woman with a kind but no-nonsense air about her, dealt with an ongoing dilemma. She didn't like to, but felt obliged to say something to old Randy Cooper. If she didn't, his delinquency on returning books would end up with some vital shelves permanently missing important authors that many others wanted to read. Randy consumed more books at a rate faster than anyone else who came to the library, and last year that was over forty thousand, many of whom came from Union City or even farther away.

No doubt of it, Randy was a far-above-average reader, and she admired that in the past three months alone he'd consumed several volumes of Marcel Proust's *Remembrance of Things Past,* had tackled *War and Peace,* and had demolished *Tess of the D'Urbervilles* and two other novels by Thomas Hardy as well.

"Have you lost all these books, Randy? I hope you haven't accidently thrown them out."

"No, no. Just forget to bring them in."

Randy was elderly, a World War II vet, one of the last of "the great generation." He moved slowly about with a walker and was obviously poor. Margaret knew he had lost a wife of many years only eighteen months ago and that he had to be close to ninety-five if not even older. He was lonely, surely reading had to be a solace, and she hated to put pressure on him, but her job was to keep the Somersville library up to the standards that had won it association awards. She had let him get away with his delinquency long enough, perhaps far too long.

She said, "Mr. Cooper, I'm sorry. But I can't let you have any further books until you bring back these six you've taken out, all of which are long overdue."

For the first time since she'd known him, he didn't complain and ask for more time. He just stared at her, his eyes watering slightly, and then awkwardly turning his walker, he shuffled slowly off within its embrace.

With an unchecked sigh of mixed sadness and relief, Margaret turned her attention to a young woman who had walked in and who all the while had been silently waiting her turn. "Can I help you?" and to her surprise found herself looking at a held-out police identification card. The woman wasn't in uniform and returned her questioning look with steadily held green-gray eyes set wide in an unsmiling face that betrayed nothing.

Carrie said, "Sergeant Driscoll, Miss Tate. I'm new on the force here. Came up from Union City. I don't believe we've met."

Flustered, Margaret Tate managed a warm smile, shook hands, and identified herself by name and as the head librarian. She had noticed Carrie walked with a slight limp, and when Carrie mentioned she'd been with the Union City police, she suddenly added things up mentally and realized this might possibly be the cop who had been in the shoot-out there, and deserved respect.

"What can I help you with, sergeant?" she said, while immediately wondering if she'd done anything wrong, not paid a parking ticket or committed some other offense, although she couldn't imagine what. Nothing came to mind. Perhaps not stopping at that stop sign on Raynes Road that nobody ever stopped at? She lived a highly circumspect life with another woman, a surgical nurse, and had for years. Recently they had married and applied for adoption of a child. Could it be that? Surely not.

Her anxious thoughts were instantly banished when Carrie said, "I'm investigating the deaths of Janet Weiss and her husband, Miss Tate."

"Oh, the suicides."

"Yes."

"How awfully unexpected and unfortunate. I can't remember anything like it ever happening in Somersville." The librarian found it difficult to keep looking back at the expressionless face of the young officer and eyes that seemed to look right through her.

"We're trying to build up some sort of profile," Carrie said, "that might show us why Janet Weiss and her husband killed themselves. From what we've so far gathered, there doesn't seem to be anything untoward in either of their lives, separately or as a long-married couple. They were even about to go on a long trip abroad. There were pamphlets on where to stay in Israel and Egypt."

"Of course. Glad to be of any help, sergeant. We didn't know him. I hear he was extremely nice. But we knew Janet well. She was a regular visitor to the library."

Carrie remembered relatively empty bookshelves in the Weiss house and said, "She read a lot, did she?"

"Read a lot? No. Not really. She came in often to use a computer. We keep three PCs for public use." The librarian came from behind the counter. "They're over there on that far wall behind our history and biography shelves."

Under Carrie's steady gaze, she couldn't help

rambling on, even though she felt she shouldn't. "Most people have turned to laptops and have their own at home, so that few come in these days to use ours. Perhaps you were thinking to see what Janet was emailing or texting?

Carrie covered her surprise. "It would help build a picture," she said. "If there's anything of hers still there."

"Oh, yes, I'm sure there is. And you're lucky, sergeant. Most library computers have an app that erases anything that a user has on it when they are finished. We haven't done that yet. Adding apps didn't seem worth the money, so we still use passwords." She offered a conspiratorial smile and a tone to match. "It's a bit illegal, I suppose, to let you look without a warrant or anything, but I think in this case we can make an exception. It's for such a good cause, and since dear Janet is dead, and you're police, well … we won't say anything."

Carrie offered back an unsmiling steady level look and waited while the librarian went on with, "Users often stored passwords to their emails with me, and I keep a little book of them for some, in case they can't remember." She produced a notebook from under the counter, thumbed pages and said, "Here you are. Janet Weiss. Her identification is SomersvilleWeiss99. Don't know what the *99* was for. Her password is Weiss126. Her name and the number of her house. Simple enough. I was always surprised she couldn't remember it."

Carrie had come to the library with only a vague hope that she might uncover something to perhaps convince Chief Ellis that the Weiss couple were far from suicidal, and had chosen the library because she thought she might get some information from the librarian. Now, and out of the blue, she found herself headed with the librarian toward a computer that she heard the librarian say Janet used quite often.

"Emails to a sister someplace, she told me," Margaret Tate said. "At least so I gathered from one of the few times I came by when she was using it. They were twins, she said, and had remained very close all their lives."

Carrie seated herself in front of the PC she was told Janet Weiss had used the most, and after being invited to make herself at home and stay as long she wished, was left. She booted up, and using the ID and password the librarian had given her, she quickly opened Janet Weiss's Outlook account.

"Jackpot," she muttered to herself, the moment the email inbox appeared on the monitor, little realizing that within minutes she would find the jackpot to be bigger and more dangerous by far than anything ever handled by the Somersville Police Department. As more emails appeared, she quickly got out her notebook.

Sixteen

HALF AN HOUR LATER, her head racing with the texting between the two sisters, Carrie shut down the PC, and after thanking the librarian, left the library without noticing the older woman who, back turned, seemed to be studiously looking for something in the index files. She was Mary Rose O'Connell and there to routinely check for news with Margaret Tate, whom she knew well. The Somersville librarian, who was a recipient of most of the town's gossip, was often a good source of legitimate news.

The moment Carrie left the computer and had paused on her way out to say good-bye to Margaret Tate, Mary Rose recognized her. Instantly suspicious as to why a police officer would be using a library computer when every sort of computer was available at the police station, and determined to discover what Carrie had been up to, she chose to remain unseen by Carrie and waited until she had left, and until another book seeker finished speaking briefly to the librarian, before turning away from the index files and approached Margaret Tate herself.

She started her quest obliquely. "That police officer. I didn't recognize her, and I know them all.

Is she new in Somersville?"

"Yes. You didn't recognize her? I didn't at first myself. But I'm sure she was the officer in the shoot-out down your way last year that you covered. She's on a working medical leave from Union City, as I understand it."

"Oh, of course." Mary Rose made a pretense of kicking herself for not at once recognizing Carrie, although she'd known full well the moment she'd seen her who Carrie was. "She was a little out of context," she said. "What was she doing here in your library? You haven't had a break-in, have you?"

Margaret laughed. "No, no. Nothing so dramatic. She just wanted to check out Janet Weiss's emails."

"The suicide case?"

"Correct."

A reporter's memory bells rang in Mary Rose's head. She had approached the rabbi at the Beth Israel Cemetery before Carrie had arrived for the funeral, and he'd said that he more or less believed Janet Weiss's and her husband's deaths had been murder, not suicide. Within hours, her paper had gone to press with that. Now here was the same cop again checking out emails. One question loomed large in Mary Rose. Why?

"Checking Emails, was she? I'd like to get a look at them myself, Margaret."

Something of a gossip she may have been, but Margaret Tate drew a line at some things she knew were not ethically right, like breaking the confidences of her patrons and gossiping about their personal lives. She said, "Sorry, Mary Rose, you know I always like to help, especially when it comes to the *Weekly Observer,* which is so important to all of us, but I can't let you do that. A cop was one thing. I could hardly refuse her, the law and all that … but … well, I hope you understand."

Mary Rose knew when to shut up. The librarian was too good a source to ever risk alienating her. She surrendered, with a put-on warm politeness she didn't really feel. "Of course, Margaret. I quite understand."

But the librarian's refusal rankled. *Where there's smoke, there's fire,* Mary Rose thought. Two sisters dead, both almost certainly homicides, and right after a week of texting that possibly had aroused police interest.

The body language and facial expression of Sergeant Driscoll when she left the library told Mary Rose, experienced in reading people, that she had indeed run into something, and that the sergeant hadn't just read texting gossip. Could the sisters have been exchanging information that was possibly about something going on at the capital?

Mary Rose's instinct for ferreting news ran deep. Okay to murder Janet in Somersville, but in the same week in the faraway state capital murder Judith, enjoying a very high-up job with the lieutenant governor? And after texting considerably with her sister? And why so much texting if Janet was to leave on holiday almost immediately afterwards? To the veteran news editor, something wasn't right.

Like every good reporter, Mary Rose had anonymous sources. One such she had often used for whatever he could offer in the way of goings-on in the state government was an accountant in the state tax office in the Capitol building. As soon as she got back to the newspaper's office in Union City, she put in a call to him.

Seventeen

"**D**AD, IT TOOK MY breath away. I was shocked, and I mean really shocked. What the hell do you think I should do? I slept lousy last night because of it."

George Driscoll, still in his pajamas and robe, unshaven and his remaining hair not yet brushed, made small rings with the bottom of his coffee mug on the paper cloth that covered the kitchen breakfast table, all the while keeping his eyes fixed on BOSS MAN, the logo etched into the mug's semi porcelain, a present from his daughter on Father's Day.

For a moment, he didn't look up at Carrie, who sat opposite him, waiting for him to speak. He'd thought her vaguely agitated when she'd come to see him and fix his breakfast, even before he'd got himself painfully out of bed. It was quite unusual. Carrie was hardly one to shirk work or screw up on jobs. What she did in any police matter was always first-class, and he had wondered why the early morning visit.

Sam Ellis had dropped by last night just to say hello and chat about old times a moment or two, and when he'd asked Sam how Carrie was doing, the aging police chief had evaded his eyes before saying, "Fine, George, Just fine. Great kid."

Was Carrie in any sort of trouble, or had Sam finally just run into the inscrutable and often insurrectionist Carrie she really was when he'd taken her on?

But this? The first thing she'd said was, "Three closely related people dead, Dad, after texting state secrets back and forth. Why? There has to be a reason other than coincidence."

She had then launched into everything, first hesitantly, then holding nothing back and pouring out all she'd had learned from the exchange of texts and emails between Judith Freedman and her sister, Janet Weiss.

Listening, George could hardly down rising anger. What he heard ran against everything he'd always held to be the semi-sacredness of the government, which, when in vicious combat in Vietnam, he believed in the oath he had sworn to protect and defend. When he finally raised his eyes, he said, "And you think the lieutenant governor or somebody found out Judith Freedman was spying on him?"

"Best reason I can find for her murder. And her sister's. National security has a long arm—someone, probably when automatically monitoring Judith's boss's cell phone, caught Judith messing about with it and decided to monitor her phone too, just in case."

"Let me ask you another question. Do you have any proof at all that the president is somehow involved in all this, or is it just surmise?"

Carrie said, "Of course I don't have proof,

but why would our governor be texting some guy named Marcus at the White House if he wasn't? The only guy in the West Wing named Marcus is Marcus Albright, the Deputy Chief of Staff, who's in the Oval Office every day. Also, there's all the closed-door meetings between our governor and Tony Mellor, the top guy in the assembly, and with the president's cozy billionaire crony Arnold Guthrie. You know who I mean—that big world-class construction guy whose money helped put the president in office. Guthrie's already put out his plans to deep-dig that abandoned iron mine south-east from here and use it for dumping atomic waste from the Orion nuclear plant they just shut down."

"He can't do that, Cass. Using that mine for waste was voted down two years ago by the state legislature. There was quite a public uproar about it."

"Sure," Carrie said. "But that was before a new legislature was voted in, right?" There was oblique sarcasm in her tone. "And guess who's going to apply political pressure on the new legislature to turn things around?"

"But that's Washington interfering in state politics."

"Exactly. Get smart, Dad. Guthrie was a major contributor to the president's election, so it's a pretty sure thing he is probably going to get what-ever he wants."

George had a last disbelieving shot.

"Where did you get all this from, Cass?"

Carrie laughed. "Starting with our public library, I put a lot of twos and twos together. I'm a detective, remember? I do real live picture puzzles."

George surrendered more or less and reluctantly. "Okay, okay. So your far-fetched idea is that the president possibly fits in, but why?"

"Corruption, Dad. Don't you see? The money. The president's campaign PAC with a billion or so in contributions, add to that millions secretly siphoned out of the military budget. That's public money going to a private construction enterprise, and you can bet a fat cut for the president himself from crony Guthrie for the finance."

A long silence was broken by George, saying, "Jesus …"

And then, nagged by a growing suspicion, "Cass, have you talked to Terry about all this?"

Carrie laughed. "Of course not, but if I had, I'm sure Terry would have zeroed in on the Washington connection at once."

George thought of Terry, his passion for politics that went far beyond his fundraising to convert the Old Mill in Union City into condos. Rumor had it that he'd soon be seen someplace in the state government and possibly one day in Washington. His daughter had hit it lucky with the young man; he was the right guy for her, but everything Carrie had said to him about what she'd learned seemed right out of Terry's book, and he hoped she was telling the truth when she denied talking to him about it. Cops shouldn't listen to outsider opinions where police work was concerned, or reveal to others what they were doing. He couldn't keep a certain truculence from his tone when he said, "I hope you didn't."

And then, when she ignored him, "Cass, what about Sam? When are you going to unload all of this on him?"

"That's just it, Dad. It's why I'm telling you instead. He pulled me off the case and all but said he'd fire me if I kept on seeing the Weiss suicides as homicides."

George said, "Just the same, Cass, you have to tell him. Look at it this way, and maybe it seems far-fetched at the moment, but you know newspaper people. Never happy until they've dug out all the dirt. If what you've learned should ever prove right and balloon publicly, there'd be the question of why Sam wasn't onto it too if one of his cops was. Like it or not, if he was to learn you knew about this all along and didn't tell him, then you'll be dead where he is concerned. One of his own cops and he didn't know? Sam's a proud man. He's known you since you wore braces, but he'll cut you loose but fast. Bet on it. You won't mean nothing to him."

George played again with his coffee cup and then said, "There's still another angle why he's got to be told. Sam is soon to sign out of police work. If you are possibly right and this is big-time corruption, and if it should balloon and him not warned, he could be forced to early retire, which would rob him of a chunk of pension.

"Besides," he added, "Would blowing a whistle really make any difference in something possibly this corrupt? After they got through with us down here, wouldn't their going right on with what they're doing make any sacrifice on your part a sick joke?"

He went silent then, letting it all hang. He suddenly felt terribly old and terribly tired, unable to cope. When he finally brought himself to speak again, he said, "Honey, I've been advising you for years, some good advice, some of it bad, some of it useful, some of it of no damned use at all. But on this one, well, I know I'm leaving you between a rock and a hard place, but it will be up to you to find out which direction to go in. And that's the way it's got to be. I just don't have it in me anymore to decide this sort of mess."

Carrie felt the blow. She had so hoped her father would somehow find a way out for her, perhaps be the one to break all she'd learned to Sam Ellis. But dismally, she knew he only half believed her and wasn't going to. His words left her suddenly feeling very alone and vulnerable. But oddly, she knew he felt the same.

She rose and planted a kiss on the top of her father's head. "Don't worry, Dad, I'll figure something," and later, while putting away the breakfast things she'd fixed, and had done the washing up, and had made up his bed, and got her father in front of his favorite morning news program, she thought, *Well, maybe it's a good thing he can't help. Damn it, I'm not sixteen any longer. I'm thirty, and a cop, and a good one. I'm supposed to figure out these things for myself, not go whining to a tired older man, or any man, as far as that goes.*

Just the same, the rest of her working day slipped by without her coming up with any solution. She dutifully tracked down the offending graffiti artist and issued him an order to appear in court on a charge of defacing public property; she tried to find anybody who might have seen the rotten business of someone dumping their garbage on another person's front lawn, and all the while going nowhere with what Judith Freedman and Janet Weiss had texted and emailed each other.

When she drove back to Union City that evening, she was dying to fill Terry in on everything she had learned. But she didn't. Way back when a rookie, she'd learned not to divulge any of her job to anyone, not even those intimately close. She had violated the rule too often where both Terry and her father were concerned, but this time she knew that what she had learned had to have a line drawn before it.

At bedtime, when she had left Terry wondering what was wrong when she refused his usually welcomed advances after they finally turned in for the night, she had decided what she must do. She wasn't going to let fear of anything allow her to betray the oaths she and Sam had taken as police officers or the one her father had taken before that when he joined the Marines. If she blew the whistle, with or without Sam, and all the Washington evil kept right on going, at least she and Sam and her father could sleep nights knowing they'd stood up for what they believed in.

Then, and slightly before she fell asleep, she thought again of Janet and Sidney Weiss, and found herself imagining two deadly intruders entering and murdering; and for some weird and inexplicable reason, if not to hide clues to their murder, dragging their bodies down across the lawn to the stone toolshed.

She thought of Judith too. Even though all three were dead, she told herself, if it was left up to her, they were still going to have their day in court.

Eighteen

ALTHOUGH BY NOW USED to merciless silences that hid even more merciless thoughts, Marcus could not remember when he had seen the president's silence more foreboding. While he and General Lansdowne sat helpless, the normal quiet of the Oval Office was made to seem even more so when punctuated only occasionally by a distant murmur of sound from somewhere beyond its walls.

Even worse than his not speaking was the physical appearance of the graying man behind the Resolute Desk, his tightly compressed lips, the unrelenting secrecy of his narrowed eyes that revealed nothing of his thinking; the rhythmical tap-tap-tap-tap of the ordinary wooden pencil he held between manicured thumb and index finger against Resolute Desk blotter was like the Chinese water torture.

When finally the president broke the silence with a single word, "So?" Lansdowne found his courage and dared to speak. "Mr. President," he said, "we will be meeting with Arrowsmith today, and unquestionably they will be able to answer your questions. As for future silence from the press, sir, I can assure you that Arrowsmith will take any step, no matter how extraordinary, to suppress it."

The president spoke again. "They, they." The ice in his voice was emphasized by its quiet. "By they, I take it you mean this imbecile McClellen running Arrowsmith, and you can perhaps ask him, if he can't completely silence the so called news in that little local rag, what he has in mind if it's poisonous reporting is picked up by the AP or CNN? What then?"

The object of the presidential fury was another news item in the *Weekly Observer* that had been inadvertently revealed to the president by a reporter's question during a routine press conference. The reporter had picked up on the news article bylined by the paper's editor, Mary Rose O'Connell. It stated that:

Police in Somersville are continuing to investigate further the so-called suicide deaths of Janet and Sidney Weiss, whose half-decomposed bodies, a near empty syringe of deadly poison on a table between them, were only discovered this spring when apparently dead last December. A detective of the Somersville police was seen today checking out a library computer Janet Weiss extensively used during the ten days before her death. Police have not yet disclosed what they found in a possible exchange of texts and emails between the deceased and her sister, who worked for the lieutenant governor at the state capital. But the potential seriousness of that exchange is possibly seen in a continued police investigation of the sisters' unexplained and possibly homicide deaths, both in the same week.

"Sir," General Lansdowne managed, "Sir, when we see McClellen, sir, I will make it very clear to him that he will have to take care of this reporter."

The president stared at Lansdowne a long moment and in a deadly silence that was again broken only by the tap-tap-tap of his pencil. When he finally spoke, it was in such a quiet voice as to send chills down Marcus's back, and then only to say, "See that you do, Lansdowne. See that you do." Nothing else.

When granted permission by the president to leave, Marcus made it back to his office to collapse in his chair. His legs felt surprisingly weak, and the blood beating in his ears was thunder. He was short of breath. His shirt, straight from the laundry, which he'd put on so confidently right before breakfast, clung to him with perspiration. For a few minutes, while he slowly regained his breath and the rapid thudding of his heart had decreased to near normal, he found himself wondering how such a plush job as he'd finally achieved could have turned into such a nightmare.

There were moments, like just now, he thought, when the price he had to pay for what the job gave him was too high. Today, come what may, he felt like typing out a letter of resignation, cleaning out his desk, and walking out of the White House without a word to anyone. A blessed obscurity beckoned, a small-town law practice, a certain divorce from Aggie. Whatever. Even a homeless pad under a bridge someplace, if that's the way he'd end up, would seem better than the stressful game he was a part of that was becoming every hour far more stressful.

A knock on his door brought him out of his

reverie, and even before he could sit upright, Lansdowne entered. "Marcus. We have Arrowsmith."

All fucking military as usual, Marcus thought, and dutifully obeyed.

Lunch, as arranged, was in a near anonymous pizza joint in the labyrinth of shops and eating places that marked the lower concourse of Union Station. Someone on Lansdowne's staff had arranged it, and Marcus cursed whoever it was. The place was small, dirty, and the air conditioning didn't work. The waitress who served them chewed gum and wiped the greasy tabletop clean with a dirty rag as they sat down.

McClellen had got there slightly before them, and his appearance surprised Marcus, who hadn't met him yet; Lansdowne had conducted original negotiations for Arrowsmith services. Expecting a mercenary soldier-of-fortune type, burly, a military haircut, a scar or two on his face, and perhaps a tattoo of a Sherman tank on his arm, he found himself facing a rather pale-faced man in his sixties who had thinning blond hair, a lightly receding chin, and was immaculately dressed in an expensively tailored suit.

Lansdowne didn't waste time on preliminaries other than to say as a way of introduction, "Marcus Albright," with a jerk of his head in Marcus's direction. He laid right in as though he had just learned a lesson from the president in forthrightness. "We have your preliminary indication of whopping costs, and we'll respond as arranged with a government investment into necessary munitions for the insurrection in Mali as a cover. I have to tell you, however, McClellen, we are not happy with your performance."

The reaction to his confrontation was a thin smile. "I take it you are referring to an article in a small-town weekly."

"What else?"

"We were not contracted, general, to supervise the media. If you want the *Weekly Observer* silenced, we will only be too happy to satisfy. But I am obliged to tell you, the next bill might be larger than the last when we investigated an exchange of damaging information between a state civil employee and a far distant retired couple. Messing about in small towns, where everyone knows everyone else's business, such as Somersville, and to a lesser extent the larger Union City, can be expensive. It's not like operating here in the capital, for example, or Chicago, or New York, or Los Angeles. A lot of extra precautions have to be taken. Trying to silence the *New York Times* or the *Washington Post,* swarming with investigative reporters, could be pretty expensive."

Marcus saw what was coming, he knew, before Lansdowne, because the general didn't lessen his manner, but demanded belligerently, "Like what?"

There was no letup in the slightly simpering yet superior smile of the Arrowsmith boss. "Let's talk money, then, general," McClellen said.

"How much?" Lansdowne demanded. He was clearly taken aback.

McClellen 's immediate answer was to produce his cell phone, punch in some figures, think an instant and then silently turn the cell screen around so first Lansdowne then Marcus could see the figure he'd come up with.

Marcus heard Lansdowne's sharp intake of breath telling him that the general obviously had been caught off guard, but he wasn't surprised himself, even though he thought they were being thoroughly gouged. They were dealing with a ruthless international mercenary and arms dealer who had no scruples of any kind and worked for whomever paid him the most, regardless of political, ideological, or religious feelings.

Lansdowne found his voice, which had lost much of its rough-rider tone. "You're crazy."

The thin smile broadened to show slightly irregular teeth. But there was no smile in McClellen's eyes, which, in contrast, had narrowed and were expressionless. "You have to be in my business," he said, his voice a near monotone. "You charge for how much work is done. Silencing people of no account in the world except to their families, if they have any, is one thing. If executed correctly, their accident or suicide of such a person leaves only a body as evidence. But silencing a news reporter that could create a stir, even though not much of one, requires, for ultimate safety, a little more. It requires complete and permanent disappearance. No body, no crime."

"That's bullshit," Lansdowne said. And Marcus knew it was pure bluff. What came next, however, even he hadn't anticipated, and it mentally pulled him up short.

McClellen smiled. "Your prerogative to think so, general. But there's more for you to dismiss if you so wish. You now have something else you didn't have before. You have police involvement. This cop, whoever he or she was, the one who was examining the computer exchanges. Forget it for the moment. We don't make foolproof guarantees, and if anything should happen to come out, no matter how much care was taken, it could come back on you like a swarm of bees. Think the Justice Department and the FBI. You don't want that."

Lansdowne said, "I take it silencing the cop is also open to renegotiating."

McClellen shrugged. "Suit yourself." He rose. "Meanwhile, general, I anticipated your agreement where the reporter is concerned. The matter there is already a working one. Meanwhile, when you make up your mind about the cop, just let me know. Marcus, pleasure to meet you."

And with that, McClellen was gone.

Nineteen

IT WAS LATE FRIDAY night and Mary Rose had finally put the paper to bed after delays due to unexpected last-minute changes in the mayor of Union City's wedding. Planned for outdoors, it had been moved inside due to a weather report of oncoming storms.

Hurrying, she got into her car for the short drive out of central Union City into its suburbs to the private Brookfield Golf Course. Once there, she wended her way along a narrow blacktop that paralleled various fairways until she reached a small development of ranch house–style condominiums only recently built on the fringes of the golf course. Six in all and set well back from the eighth green, they were separated by tailored hedges and far enough apart to guarantee each a certain amount of privacy, and all boasted air conditioning, a washer and dryer, and a modern kitchen.

Mary Rose's, the last in a line, was a two-bedroom one. She had put herself in debt to buy it, and as her long days were always spent away from it, she was never bothered on weekends when she was at home by what she termed the ridiculous sight of what seemed an almost endless stream of golf carts along what amounted to the condo's front lawn.

Pulling up before it, she locked her car and let herself in the front door to the foyer, where she dumped her keys into a large ceramic bowl on a table and her bag and a tote crammed with a file of office memos to study over the weekend on the chair beside it.

She was flooded, as she did, with the same sense of well-being she always felt at the end of a week. Thousands of people in both Union City and in Somersville along with two other lesser towns in the area would this coming weekend be fully acquainted with what was going on in their mostly local world as against the far bigger world beyond.

Knowing it always let Mary Rose indulge in a flush of inner pleasure that she shared with no one but herself, unless to some degree her immediate assistant editor, Nate Wolkowski, a young man whose backup work to hers had in the past few years proved invaluable.

Local newspapers were going out of business everywhere across the country. Not so the *Weekly Observer.* Its affairs were in order. It owed no money and to date was comfortably in the black. Her own fastidious management had made this possible. She'd cut back on staff and got on without those gone, she'd promoted advertising, she'd increased subscriptions.

Pausing a moment to look at herself in the mirror that hung above the foyer table, Mary Rose's attention was drawn at once to the wrinkles at the corners of both eyes.

"Damn crow's feet," she muttered, and reminded herself once more to ask one of the girls at the office for the name of the product she had mentioned that was supposed to eliminate them.

With a sigh of hopelessness, she gave up on the endless struggle not to think she was no longer young and went into the living room. Retrieving from a small wine rack an excellent bottle of Chianti that she had purchased only the day before, she poured herself a glass, which she set on the low marble-topped table before the couch that, along with an easy chair and a sideboard, made up the only furniture of the room, unless framed prints of Wyeth landscapes on the walls could be counted.

Plunked down, she switched on the television so she could look at what was occurring in her current favorite PBS serial drama.

She had hardly got settled when her cell rang. She had kept it close, as always, and it was on the couch right next to her. She picked it up in an automatic unthinking flash even before she could feel annoyed at being disturbed.

"Mary Rose. Who's calling?"

"It's me, Nate."

"Nate? Doesn't sound like you."

"It's my cell. I'm in an odd place. There's been a nasty accident."

"Oh? Where?" Mary Rose came instantly alert.

"Gas explosion over on Fourth Street. I think the building next to the pharmacy there."

Mary Rose was already up off the couch before she spoke. "I'm on my way," she said, and as an afterthought, rapidly downed the still mostly full glass of chianti before she headed for the door, grabbing up her handbag and car keys on the way.

Reaching her car, parked conveniently near her condo's front door, she yanked open the driver's side door, slid rapidly behind the wheel, put on her seat belt, and started the motor. The sound of it coming to life almost extinguished another sound—a rushed movement around her head and shoulders as two gloved hands reached over her from the back seat and snapped duct tape firmly across her mouth before she could emit even a startled gasp. Moaning in instant shock and bewilderment, she felt her seat belt unfastened, and she was dragged bodily from the car. Slammed down on the pavement, her arms were yanked behind her back, her wrists were tied together with plastic cord, and still struggling to understand what was happening to her, she was tossed doubled over into the yawning trunk of her car.

The trunk lid shut, she felt rather than heard two doors slam shut, one the driver's, the other on the passenger's side. The car's motor started, and for the first time, bewilderment and shock began to be replaced with a mounting terror. What had happened? Where was she? Pain crept over her whole cramped body, tortured her arms and wrists. Her taped mouth stifled and made her gag on her own vomit that surged up uncontrolled. There was the suffocating smell of gasoline and oily rags.

Vaguely she heard men's voices. Talking. There was a burst of laughter, then silence, save for the hum of the car's motor and tires. She was being driven somewhere. But where? And why?

It seemed forever before the whine of the tires suddenly ceased, with her being abruptly rolled against the front of the trunk as the car stopped. She heard laughing and shouting and music not far off, and tried to scream, and couldn't. The duct tape across her mouth choked. There were the muffled sounds of the two men talking. One of them cursed, she heard the other saying something she thought was, "Kids these days; they party everywhere."

Then the car moved again, accelerating, its tires whining once more. She tried to understand where she was until quite quickly the car slowed fast again and abruptly stopped, rolling her forward hard.

The car's doors opened and shut. Moments later, fresh air rushed about her as the lid of the trunk was opened. Rough hands seized her. A man's voice said, "Shit, she's fucking pissed herself," and she realized in horror that she'd urinated.

In the darkness, she tried to see where she was, but her only impression was the rough cracked cement that she was being half carried, half dragged over. She felt the open air of night, heard faraway night sounds, a distant car, the low hum of a city still partially awake. Then sound ceased, and there was a dead stillness and a darkness darker than night. Flashlight beams raked about, hit her eyes, blinding, before sweeping away. Suddenly she was pulled upright and slammed down against something rigidly hard, and then facedown on a concrete floor. Through a sea of pain, she heard the men again.

"Okay, she's safe enough here. I'm for coffee."

"We passed a diner on the way."

"Let's go, then. Kids will give it up in an hour or so." And then closer to her, "Hey, lady, get some sleep. we'll be back."

Laughter as they turned away. Flashlight beams waved about. One landed on one of the two men. A fleeting glimpse that he was tall and wore a suit, her surprise that he looked like any businessman before the light dashed away and focused on what seemed to be machinery, until inky darkness rushed around her again and with it silence, save for the distant sound of her car engine starting and a rush of water from a stream someplace.

Pain, nausea came and went for what seemed forever, waves of it, one wave after another. She slept and woke and slept again, and then the men came back, flashlights sweeping what she saw was a vast cavernous room around her, it's celling hung with belts and pulleys, and below them massive machinery of some kind. Very slowly she realized she'd been here before. It was a place she'd written about when shown around by the young guy who had talked about condos.

She didn't have time to think further. She was heaved to her feet, dragged outside, back across the broken concrete, dumped again into the car's trunk.

The car accelerated forward. Its tires moaned. Where was it going now? But then, after what seemed a short while, it stopped. Doors opened, then shut; she heard voices very close. A rush of cool night air all around her again as the lid of the trunk was opened. A moment of excruciating pain that shot through her whole being as she was lifted up by her tortured arms and dumped face down and hard, to be enveloped by a smell of wet grass and earth.

Flashlights again and a new wave of emotion, bewilderment, as she realized she was seeing close-by tombstones. She was in a cemetery. She saw a plastic sheet unfolded and laid down near her. There was complete silence until broken by some sound she at first couldn't identify. Was it a shovel digging up dirt? It went on and on and on, mingled now and then with men's heavy breathing and curses. She heard one say, "Looked around. Kids left one hell of a mess. Glad we don't have to clean it up. Bottles, paper plates, plastic utensils everywhere. Some of them tossed up."

She lost track of time. And then one man's voice said, "Good enough. Get hold of her."

She felt hands around her ankles, other hands grasping her neck and hair. She felt lifted past a pile of dirt on the plastic sheet, and then dropped again, A brief sense of falling, her face hit hard into now dry earth. She heard the clank of the shovel again as it lifted rocks and dirt, and then the weight of what the shovel had dug dropped onto her legs. She had only begun to realize that she was being buried when a heavy shovel full of rocks and dirt smashed down onto her face. She tried to breathe to scream through the duct tape, couldn't.

More dirt, shovelful after shovelful covered Mary Rose. Her body heaved a little for a moment or two and then was still. After a while there was only the sounds of the nighttime woods around where she lay buried. One of the two men took away the plastic sheet. There was the flick of a lighter as the other lit a cigarette.

One of the men said, "Hurry it up."

The other dragged away the plastic sheet and its load of dirt, came back a few minutes later, and said, "Okay. Let's go."

In the very far distance, there was a momentary glow of another kind of light in the sky and then the faint rumble of thunder. The car's doors slammed. Its motor started, and as the first few drops of rain began to fall, the car drove back out of the cemetery.

Twenty

IN THE KITCHEN OF George Driscoll's small home, Police Chief Sam Ellis shifted uncomfortably in his chair and toyed uneasily with his coffee mug. He'd been seated with his many years' friend George for more than half an hour talking over old times, and he still hadn't got to the real reason for his visit. He felt in an almost impossible to solve dilemma when George suddenly wheeled back from the sink where he had been refilling the coffee pot and said, "Sam. You didn't just come to see me to talk over old times. Something's troubling you. Come on, now. Out with it."

Finally revealed, Sam, didn't know whether to feel relieved or even more acutely uncomfortable. But there it was at last, and he was stuck with it. He took a gulp of the coffee in his mug that had already started to grow cold and said, "Yeah, you're right, George. I've got a real problem at work that I was really hesitant to tell you about. But here it is." He cleared his throat took a breath and said, "It's your daughter."

"Carrie?" George didn't try to hide his surprise. Although he at once suspected what was to come. He said perfunctorily, "What's up, then? Spill it."

"She's got it in her head," Sam said, "for some

"

darned reason or other, that Janet and Sid Weiss didn't kill themselves. That they were murdered. And she's assembled some sort of half-baked evidence that wouldn't hold up in any court in the land for five seconds to try to convince me that she's right. That's okay, I guess. She's entitled to her opinion, but even after I told her no-go under any circumstances, she's kept right on investigating and digging up what I'm sure will be even more nonsense. Herman told me she was over to the library sniffing around this morning. Straight insubordination, George. You wouldn't put up with it if the police department was yours, and I can't either.

"But hold on, there's more, a lot more. And it's not good." He drank the last of his coffee and then said, "It's this. I got a call today from the office of the Police Supervision up at the capital. I don't know how they managed to hear Carrie was carrying on, but they said she'd been at the library a few days back, last week, I think, asking questions and insinuating she was investigating a homicide. And for some damned reason it's hands off. They didn't say why, although I asked. They just said it came from above."

"That it came from above?"

"That's right."

"And they didn't say who?"

"Right again."

Except for emitting a low whistle, George Driscoll remained silent. He wheeled around to a get out a bottle of Jack Daniel's from a cabinet. Bringing it back to the table he poured both himself and Sam a double shot. He said, "Okay, you've relieved your mind, Sam, now it's my turn. Drink up, because you're going to need it, and don't interrupt me until I'm finished, okay?"

When Sam shrugged and nodded, "Sure, go ahead, George," George started right off, wasting no words.

"First of all, Sam," he said, "while I understand why you rejected Carrie's evidence as nonsense—I probably would have done the same—you're dead wrong. It isn't nonsense. The Weiss couple did not commit suicide as everyone, including the coroner, said. They were murdered." He held up a stilling hand, "Wait. Listen." And then, "Carrie came to see me yesterday at breakfast time, and she was real upset. Never saw her like that in all the years I raised her. Wanted my advice as to what to do about what she'd learned looking into a computer exchange of emails and texting between Janet Weiss and her sister, Judith, who works for the lieutenant governor up at the state capitol."

George paused to put back a swallow of Jack Daniel's and then told Sam exactly what Carrie had told him she'd run into. "Corruption, Sam," he said, "And big time, apparently. Dumping atomic waste into the old mine that the legislature voted against before they got voted out, and using public money to do it. Messages back and forth between the sisters seeming to say it could even involve the president. If so, that would sure explain as to why, if somebody had somehow got onto them knowing, both sisters ended up dead.

"And there's also your reason, Sam, for Police Supervision coming down on your head. Some rotten bastard in Washington scared we might unearth something down here they don't want unearthed, and putting the scrunch on us via one of our state biggies—my guess: our own pet reptile, the secretary of state. Always looking for a way, that one, to curry political favor."

After that, neither said a word for a while until, in a voice slightly strained from the shock he felt, Sam asked, "You said Carrie came looking for your advice. What did you tell her?"

"Didn't. Couldn't. Left it up to her."

"And that leaves it up to me, I suppose," Sam said. He shifted his young-no-longer body about in his chair, took another swallow of Jack Daniel's, and there was a long silence before he spoke. When he finally broke it, he said, "George, my grandparents came over to this country because they believed in what they'd always heard it stood for."

Sam paused a moment before he continued. Then he said, "Their name wasn't Ellis, it was Elitovsky, and they came from a dictatorship where the dictator was the law. What most appealed to them about the United States, their new country, was that nobody was above the law, not even the president. That feeling sort of stuck in the family down through the years, and I guess it landed finally on me. I may run a small-town police force, George, but I'll be damned if I'm going to let the President of the United States, or anybody else in Washington who's breaking the law, threaten me not to expose them. Your daughter is a first-rate detective, and as far as I'm concerned, she can go right on investigating. I'll take the rap for it."

George poured them each another round of Jack Daniel's.

Twenty-One

WAKING, CARRIE REMEMBERED SHE had an impossible day ahead, and she lay without stirring for a few minutes, almost overwhelmed with nervous anticipation. She couldn't stop thinking, just as she couldn't half her sleepless night, about what she'd learned reading the texts that had flowed back and forth between Janet Weiss and her sister, Judith Freedman, at the far-off state capital.

Like it or not, she was going to tell Sam Ellis. What she'd collected at the library made her disobeying orders and the possible humiliation of losing her badge and gun along with her job completely unimportant. A nothing. It wasn't as though he wouldn't learn of the computer revelation sooner or later. Of course he would. Somehow. She didn't know how, but Somersville was a small place, and somebody would talk. The librarian? Somebody else? And the truth would out, and he would have been kept in the dark by one of his own cops while his job and with it his old-age pension were possibly jeopardized.

She glanced at her bedside clock. It said six. She and Terry hadn't called it quits last night until nearly midnight, drinking wine, with his realizing something was wrong and trying to find out what it was, and her refusing to tell him. By turning-out-lights time, they weren't speaking.

He lay besides her now still in a dead sleep. His current work schedule, like hers, was these days a minimum of ten or eleven hours a day, and on weekends he had the whole business of hoping to turn the Old Mill into condos and a mall on top of it. She kissed one of his hands that stuck out from under the sheets, then rose, careful not to disturb his sleep, and got herself dressed, strapping her holstered Glock semiautomatic along with her other gear firmly around her waist.

She didn't dare make coffee. The bubbling coffee machine made a terrible racket, enough to wake the dead. She'd always meant to buy a new one, but had yielded to Terry's frugal insistence that they make do—they couldn't afford luxury of any kind. She silently got some orange juice from the fridge and poured herself a glass. It would have to do until she got to Somersville, where she could pick up coffee at the Lunch Pail.

Driving the thirty miles there in her and Terry's ten-year-old Toyota, which he somehow managed with some sort of magic to keep running, she was almost glad she'd risen extra early. The long, nearly straight blacktopped highway was almost void of any traffic, and getting to the office before anyone else would mean she probably wouldn't have to face Ellis first thing.

But pulling into the nearly empty parking lot before the fire station and the police office, coffee container now filled at the Lunch Pail on the seat beside her, her heart sank. Sam Ellis's old Buick sedan was already there, parked in its usual place at the end of the line of the force's six police cars. Worse, as she got out of her car, she thought she saw the chief standing at the window of his office. Too late to back out now, she thought. And tried to urge on her courage, which had started to lag. *C'mon, Carrie. Don't think, just do it. You're not a criminal; you're a cop.* She went into the empty office and sat down and waited.

But Chief Ellis made no appearance until other officers on duty that day had entered and awaited orders. When he gave them, it was brief. His eyes slowly swept the assembly and said, "Okay. For today, Pete takes traffic, Andy high school duty, Jon middle school, and Clarence, you'd best get over to elementary. Two of you cruise-check the whole town to right out past the dump, decide between you who takes what part, and the rest of you standby on call. Carrie, I want to see you in my office."

As abruptly as he had appeared, he left the room. Herman Miller smirked at Carrie as she rose to follow the chief. "Suspect you got it coming to you, smart ass."

She ignored him. This was it. She'd let him say whatever he had in mind, and then she'd tell him.

Entering the chief's office, she found him swiveled around on his chair and staring out the window. "Carrie, sit down," he said, the moment she quietly closed the door. When her chair legs scraping the floor told him she had, he swiveled back. For what seemed forever, he stared at her, making it hard for Carrie to meet his eyes.

Then he said, "Carrie, I owe you an apology. I saw your dad last night. We had a few drinks together for old times' sake, and he brought me up to date on how far you had got on the Weiss suicides actually being homicide. And yes, I heard it all, including the whole dirty business of dumping atomic waste into the old mine you picked up on, along with Washington being involved.

"I want you to keep on with your work on it, Carrie, and for the moment here with me. If things explode in any way, you might be better off with Tom Parrier back down at Union City, and I'll be happy to surrender you if he asks. You're here only temporarily anyway. Meanwhile, get me proof of the homicides this end, and a suspect if possible. Keep me posted, and don't hesitate to ask me for any help you might need.

"If it's forensics, I'll talk to Amery Rutgers, bossing things with the state police. If needs be, he can send down a crime scene investigations unit. Just ask for it and it's yours. I should call down a CSI anyway. It would be a good idea if one of the killers had left DNA someplace in the Weiss house. You can never tell. Even the best of the bastards slips up occasionally. Meanwhile, Carrie, enlist that jackass Miller out there to do any work you want done that you can't handle alone. Got that? On your way out, tell him I'd like to see him a moment."

Almost speechless, Carrie managed a "Yes, sir."

"Good. Now skedaddle. It's a working day." The chief began to busy himself with papers scattered on his desk, but when Carrie got to the door, he looked back up at her and said, "And Carrie?"

"Sir?

"Three murders, and I think probably, as I'm sure you do, that they are linked. Whoever it is who's involved—they're dangerous. Be careful. Watch your back." And with a faint smile, "Don't want any grieving fathers coming around here."

"Yes, sir."

Leaving the office, she passed Herman Miller now at his desk, his feet up, enjoying coffee. He wore a smirk on his face. Carrie jerked a thumb at Chief Ellis's office and said only, "Your turn." The smirk disappeared.

At her own desk and ignoring the questioning looks of the three officers who were on standby, she sought to add it all up, and felt a little overwhelmed. First, because she was clearly exonerated, she was filled with relief. Second, when she finally cleared her head to think rationally, her thought was, *Where do I go from here?* She had no idea. Searching the Weiss's home had produced nothing; reading the sisters' texting and emails had revealed a nightmare, but nothing she could go on in trying to nail some clearly guilty murderer.

She'd been sitting silently for several minutes before she noticed a scrawled phone number she didn't recognize on her desk notepad. Puzzled, she had picked it up when one of the officers, walking past her desk on his way out, said, "That's some guy who called while you were with Ellis. Said it was important."

Carrie punched in the number on her cell. It rang and a man's voice said, "Nate Wolkowski, *Weekly Observer.*"

Carrie said, "Hi, Nate. You called me. Sergeant Driscoll, Somersville Police."

"Ah, yes, sergeant, I did. I think there's something you might want to know."

When they'd hung up, Carrie saw from the small flashing light on the extension bank on her phone that Sam Ellis was talking on his. She ought to speak to him first, brief him on what Nate Wolkowski had been on about. But there wasn't time. Five minutes later, she was in a police car and, clearing slow pokes from the road ahead with her siren and flashing blue-and-red roof lights, was on her way back to Union City.

It had only just turned eight o'clock, and the world was waking up.

Twenty-Two

THE NEWSROOM OF THE *Weekly Observer* was noisily busy when Carrie walked in unannounced. Reporters and subeditors, along with various columnists, were at their desks, hunched over their computers as they rushed, as usual on a Thursday, to meet deadlines with their end-of-the-week news and opinions. Others were equally busy writing up classified ads so important to so many of the paper's readers, along with the latest in weddings and funerals.

Two of those close to the door who had taken a break to enjoy coffee and a snack, and were pushed back from their desks talking, were the first to see her.

Surprised at the sudden and unexpected appearance of the law, so out of context from the noisy and intense atmosphere of the newsroom, they both took it upon themselves to express feigned delight at the unexpected police presence.

"Well, well, look who's here. Nothing less than the law and just in time for coffee," came from one.

And from the other, who threw both hands up in mock surrender, "Not guilty, lady. Put away the handcuffs."

A silent, icy stare from Carrie cut off any further

comment until finally one of the two decided her presence might demand seriousness. "Yes, ma'am. Can I help?"

Carrie had just decided to answer when Nate Wolkowski appeared at a door whose glass panel announced was the realm of EDITOR. As he also stared in equal surprise, Carrie brushed past the two reporters and said, "Hi, Nate. We have things to discuss." And making her way through the suddenly hushed newsroom, she pushed past him into the small functional room from which Mary Rose had run the newspaper. "I'm all ears," she said, and promptly dropped into a chair.

Slightly nonplussed, Nate followed her in and closed the door, isolating them, went to sit at the desk, and said apologetically, "Sorry for those two out there." And then, realizing why she had to be there and further collecting himself, said, "Mary Rose. I waited two days, and when she still didn't show up, I started running the paper myself. Maybe I'm not supposed to, but somebody had to." He stopped nervously and then said, "It's not like her. I hope she's not sick or in some kind of trouble."

"I hear you," Carrie said. "But why call me? What's wrong with your own Union City cops?"

Nate shifted uncomfortably. "Well, for all I know she took off to Las Vegas or someplace on a holiday and could walk back in here as though nothing had happened to cause any worry. We met a couple of times when you were down here, and so I sort of felt I had a friend in the police who I could talk to first in case it's all nothing and it ends up with her turning up mad as hell because of cop involvement, and with me at the police station explaining a missing person alarm. I didn't know you'd transferred to Somersville."

Carrie tried not to reveal her curiosity. She said, "You've been seeing too many crime movies. If she's really gone missing, you'll have to report it here, like it or not. Any delay could drop you in the deep, okay? So let me ask you a few questions. When did you last see her?"

"I told you on the phone. Two days ago. When we packed in the office, around six thirty."

"Did she give you any indication of where she was going, or say anything unusual?"

"Only that she was beat and going straight home, to put her feet up, have a drink, and watch the TV news. Something like that."

"Did you check her home?"

"Yes. She has a condo over by the Brookfield Golf Course."

"Brookfield. The fancy private one."

"Yes."

"And?"

"Well, her car was still there, so I guess that's what bugged me."

"Did you ring her bell?"

"Yeah. A dozen times. I found a janitor, works all the condos, not just hers. He said he hadn't seen her."

"And?"

Nate looked sheepish. "Well, I guess I probably shouldn't have, but I talked him into letting me into her condo. I looked around quickly, but didn't see anything unusual. Her car keys were in a bowl in the foyer. It was like she just suddenly upped and walked out. There was an unfinished glass of wine on a table in front of the couch, and the TV was running."

Carrie thought a moment. Lucky for Nate he hadn't found Mary Rose dead. There was every chance her not showing up for work or answering her phone was because she'd been stricken by a heart attack.

Then another, far more serious thought quickly followed. Three people had died because apparently they had learned of a high-level conspiracy involving the disposal of nuclear waste. Mary Rose had clearly been smelling around; she'd written two columns now insinuating Washington involvement, although she hadn't said how or why. Had she possibly somehow run into the same information Judith and her sister had discovered and fatally shared?

She said to Nate, "Nate, there could be things here that I can't discuss with you, but you were smart to bring me in on your worry."

"So, what do I do now?"

"You don't. You sit tight and run the newspaper until I've had a word with your Union City cops. Meantime, Nate, nothing in print, okay? Not one word about Mary Rose missing. Got that?"

On the way to the Union City police station, Carrie kept thinking of Mary Rose's car keys in a bowl, the TV running, and an unfinished glass of wine. Nothing about it sounded good.

Twenty-Three

THE UNION CITY FORCE was triple that of Somersville's. Besides the city itself, its thirty-four cops covered a far larger rural area around it and provided police protection for several towns too small to support their own police. A large, busy place, located near the town hall in a modest modern building, it was quickly identified by the often dozen police cruisers parked in front of it as well as the modest sign over its front door saying POLICE.

After parking her Somersville police cruiser and entering, Carrie went directly upstairs to the busy second-floor detective department, and as she went, enjoyed a pleasant feeling of the familiar. It had been home to her for eight years and nearly everyone there was a good friend. Half a dozen desks were occupied by cops busy at computers, other desks by clerical workers. There were several closed-off offices, one housing Tom Parrier, the chief. A corridor at the room's end led to stairs down to a holding cell, an interview room, and the undecorated working area that was the domain of the desk sergeant, there to book arrests and those being detained as well as a temporary resting place for uniformed officers coming and going from duty throughout the city.

Carrie's entry created a stir, and she was greeted like a long-lost friend. "Hey, look who's here." And, "Hey, Carrie, how's it going?" And, "What's with our favorite gunslinger?" Several began to applaud. The noise brought Tom Parrier from his office. The chief, at forty-five, was a dark-haired veteran of the war in Iraq with the forever quick intelligent all-embracing look and build of an NFL quarterback.

"Carrie? What a pleasant surprise. What's up?" A broad smile lit Parrier's face.

In answer, Carrie nodded at his office and said, "Got a few minutes?"

"For you, the whole morning, if you want." He told the clamoring gang they would have to wait for a second shot at her, showed her into his office, and closed the door. "What's going on, Carrie? And how's the bullet?"

Carrie said, "It's there."

He laughed. "I see it didn't stop your never mincing any words." And then, "So. Anything serious?"

"It might be," she said and told him. All of it, and in detail, beginning with Mary Rose and what seemed to be a missing person case; her first conviction that it was but now a suspicion it wasn't. She told him about the Weiss suicides she thought were clearly homicides. She told him of what she'd picked up on the computer exchange between the two sisters that indicated the one killed by a hit-and-run driver could well have been a murder as well. She told him of her reasons for suspecting Washington involvement in possible atomic waste dumping, the same as she'd told her father and Chief Ellis, and lastly, she told him of the pressure on Chief Ellis from the Police Supervisor office at the capital.

When she finished, Tom Parrier looked up from the notes he'd been making while she talked, and broke a long silence. "Quite a chase, sergeant. I'm impressed. Does Chief Ellis know you're here?"

"No, sir, I didn't have time to tell him, but he's backing me all the way."

"You said you talked to Mary Rose's second, Nate Wolkowski?"

"Yes, sir. He called me, mostly as a friend, and it's why I came down. I told him to clamp it until we know whether she's actually missing or not. I think he's okay, but I can't guarantee anybody else on the paper keeping their mouths shut."

Parrier said, "Leave that to me." He scrawled another note and then said, "Among the other things you've been telling me, Carrie, is that you think Mary Rose apparently disappearing is tied into all three deaths. Well, I think you are possibly right enough to make it worth pursuing.

"But this is your investigation, and if you want to go on with it, you're going to need more help than you'll ever get from Herman Miller. That means you should consider coming back here, which is where I suspect you'd now like to be anyway, right?"

It brought Carrie up short. She realized she hadn't really considered returning to Union City. Did she? She'd only just started to feel comfortable at Somersville.

Not waiting for an answer, Parrier quickly scrawled a reminder. When he looked up, he smiled and said, "I'm going to take your thinking about it as a yes. I'll talk to Ellis." And then, "So where do we start? You're going to need help. This may not turn out to be a one-woman show, so I think I'll team you with Inspector Irene Chagas. She's new, only here a few weeks but fitting in nicely, and in charge of our detective division. Came down from the state capital where she served as a DI in its large force and worked with their CSI crime scene investigation unit.

"She's here in sort of a last job before retirement in a year or so because she resigned to avoid suspension at state after a false charge of manslaughter. She'd unloaded her Beretta on a guy she said was coming at her with a knife, but the review board didn't agree, unfortunately for her. Politics, nothing less. We all get our load of it from time to time. I think you might make a good team and work well together. Okay by you? You've already got three murders on your hands, and hopefully not a fourth with Mary Rose."

Surprised by Parrier's forcefulness, Carrie realized she was back at Union City, like it or not. She'd barely got out, "Sure, whatever," when Parrier rose and opening the office door called out, "Irene? Spare a moment?"

And Carrie, waiting for the new DI to appear, realized she'd once again been outranked, although she couldn't believe the woman could be like Herman Miller; nobody could be that bad. She had already begun wondering where they would start looking for Mary Rose and hoping they wouldn't find her dead when she heard, "Yeah, chief?" and found herself looking at the woman she'd been told she'd be partnered with.

Twenty-Four

CARRIE DIDN'T KNOW WHAT exactly she had expected when Irene Chagas came into the office, but it wasn't a very tall, lanky older woman whose clothes somehow seemed a little on the small side—sleeves too short revealed long bony wrists—and whose long, almost horselike face was emphasized by slightly prominent teeth. She wore faded corduroy pants, a snub nosed compact nine-millimeter Beretta holstered high under her left arm, and a small gold crucifix on a chain was visible behind the several undone top buttons of her blue work shirt.

Tom Parrier introduced her, explaining that Carrie was with the Somersville force but until two months ago had been in Union City until injured during a robbery. "She caught a bullet," he said matter-of-factly.

There was no reaction from Irene. She had remained silent, save for a few perfunctory words when introduced to Carrie. Tom said, "Irene, Carrie will brief you on what's up. No point in my going into it. She's involved already more than anyone else."

And Irene spoke for the first time. "Who is Herman Miller?"

It was completely out of context and Carrie and Parrier exchanged a surprised look, and both laughed. "You've heard of him? He's theoretically the Detective at Somersville. Or was until Carrie went up there."

Irene said, "He applied to the capital force and got turned down cold."

"Figures," Parrier said. "Carrie, stay clear of Herm if you can. You, too, Irene. He's likely to put a left foot in the works. Meeting closed."

At the door seeing both women out, he shouted at the room in general, "Someone, get Carrie's old desk set up for her," and Carrie was on her own with Irene, who pulled out the chair at her own desk, sat down, got out her notebook, said simply, "Go ahead," and waited silently.

A little taken aback by her abruptness and left awkwardly standing, Carrie said, "It started up at the state capital." She went on from there, carefully outlining everything she had told Tom Parrier, from the deaths of the Weiss couple to Mary Rose's disappearing.

Throughout, Irene showed no particular interest in her longish face. She remained silent, occasionally making notes and not speaking until Carrie had finished. Then she had short questions of never more than a few words to which Carrie's answers were equally short. The Weiss home—any DNA or prints coverage? No. The same at Judith's office or apartment? No. Mary Rose—interviews with relatives or friends? No. Background financial checks? No.

And then, sarcastically incredulous, "Were there not even any forensics on the Weiss stone shed murders?"

"No."

"Why not?"

"There was an immediate decision of suicides."

"By whom?

"Chief Ellis, Herm Miller, the coroner."

Carrie stifled a sigh of relief when Irene finally announced she'd ask no more questions by pointedly snapping shut her notebook. She felt embarrassed at how little had been done in the way of investigating all three of the deaths, even though until a day ago her hands had been tied by Sam Ellis. In all, the questioning by her new DI had been so abrupt as to seem almost hostile, and Carrie, finding herself somehow on the defensive, had hardly felt like responding with anything but the briefest explanation.

She had only just begun to wonder what new side of her so-called partner she'd see next when Irene abruptly rose and said, "I don't ever work as a team. You can have your Weiss pair and Mary Rose. I'll handle the Judith hit-and-run case. Keep in touch if you must." She waved her cell phone as emphasis before pocketing it, grabbed up her handbag from where it hung by its strap on the back of her chair, transferred it to her shoulder, nodded curtly and walked out of the office.

And fuck you too, Carrie thought, and watching the office door close on the tall lank form of the detective. Being a partner with the woman was a joke. What was Tom Parrier thinking, putting them together? Had he tied her to a more experienced boss with a higher rank because he distrusted her to handle the case alone? The thought tanked her a little. It was like being told she might not have a case at all. And did Parrier know of the DI's hostility about working with others? Or until now, because she was relatively new on the Union City force, had the occasion for her to partner with someone never have arisen?

As she prepared to follow Irene Chagas out of the meeting and Tom, after asking how she felt about Irene, had said, "She's total cop, Carrie, the best," Carrie had thought something quite different. While she'd lied and smiled and said, "We're fine together," she'd been thinking, "Bitch."

Suddenly wishing she were back at Somersville, for all the depressing drawbacks of Herman Miller, Carrie went to her old office desk. She didn't think she could stand much more of her so-called partner's negative attitude, lack of respect, and speaking in monosyllables.

A stab of pain that unexpectedly lanced upward from her thigh took her mind off her new immediate boss and remembering that she had a date in two months' time to have the bullet removed, she began to add up the future of the case. So much to do, she thought, and so little to work with. She was going to have to move ahead like hell if she was to wrap up her part of the job by then.

Twenty-Five

ON THE VERY LONG day's drive to where she would start to investigate the now mostly forgotten death of one Judith Freedman, Irene Chagas found herself wishing she'd hadn't been assigned anyone to work with. And she was further unhappy that she had a sergeant on her hands who may have achieved status in Union City but had little, if any, big-force experience and had only made sergeant a year or so ago. In her own experience, it took at least six or eight years for any detective to build enough know-how to make them worthwhile. This Driscoll kid hadn't even a quarter of the number of difficult cases as someone like herself.

Irene had done her homework on the capital. Before leaving Union City, she'd spent several long hours, even though she'd worked there, renewing her acquaintance with street maps and the various often widespread locations of official government buildings. She also had gone extensively into whatever background information she could google on nearly every official of importance at work in the capitol building itself, especially concentrating on the governor and the lieutenant governor and on politically powerful Tony Mellor, the head of the legislative assembly. What were their earnings?

What were their political backgrounds—illicit affairs or long-buried trouble with the law—as well as current leanings that might have left them open to blackmail?

Two days after being "partnered" with Carrie—a term she dismissed in utter disdain, preferring to think "stuck with," Irene arrived at the state capital. She checked into an inexpensive hotel, got herself a good night's sleep after checking her favorite late night TV show, and started right off first thing in the morning with coffee at a nearby lunch counter, and going over all the notes she'd made on the case.

Mid-morning, she produced a name and an address on her iPad, made a phone call, and at noon headed for a bar with which she had a long familiarity. There she met Andrew German, a veteran detective with a pro wrestler's appearance and a former colleague.

"Shit-fire, Irene," German said," the moment they'd embraced and ordered drinks, "You could have come to the office. Been welcome there."

"No way, Andy," Irene said. "The one thing I learned in all the years working with you is that you can't go back. I may have friends in the city force, but I also have enemies. I'm not about to give them the pleasure of seeing me as food for any more gossip than I already had thrown my way."

German sympathized, and they exchanged a few memories, then he got to the point with a "So, what's up, then?"

Irene knocked back the beer she'd ordered

as chaser for a shot and launched in. She needed information, and he had to be her primary source, but she didn't want to get bogged down in a double investigation that would inhibit her end and, since he was capital police force, might even land the whole business in his hands, detrimental to herself and the Union City force. She said, "We're looking for information about the death of that pre-Christmas hit-and-run victim, right in front of the Capitol building; you'll remember it, I'm sure. The victim was Judith Freedman, an assistant to the lieutenant governor. But I'm not here for any reason you'd think. What concerns us is her sister Janet Weiss, who lived in a town named Somersville that's in the Union City orbit. I never worked on the case up here, but I know you did, and I've been sent up to gather any personal information you might have about Judith that could help us explain sister Janet's death, which is officially listed as a suicide."

German wasn't very bright, but he also wasn't stupid. He knew he wasn't hearing it all, and that Irene was covering what she was really there for. But for auld lang syne he figured it wouldn't cost him to play along. "A sister, Janet, you say?"

"You might have heard about her. Died along with her husband, about the same time as your hit-and-run here."

"And you think there's a connection?"

"Only possibly," Irene lied, aware as she did that German had to know she was covering but had decided to go along with it. "This case I'm stuck with," she said, "is just what I said. It's nothing more than a suicide. But shit almighty, Andy," she put on an air of aggrievement, "you know how things sometimes go. I've got a fucking over-meticulous new chief who wants no stone unturned even when a case is open-and-shut obvious. In this case he's got me investigating, he insists on wasting his department's time with some crazy idea that the community needs to know the why of a suicide: that everyone has the right to know. As if it's any of their goddamned business."

She shrugged as though helpless. "Whatever, it's out of my hands. I just take orders, but with a little help from you on what you came up with in the sister's hit-and-run, and I can go home tomorrow."

It worked. "Don't we all get shit like this thrown at us?" he said, stifling curiosity as to what was really going on and proving helpful. Knowing the truth wasn't going to benefit him, and someday he might need a returned favor. So, an hour later, Irene departed with a notebook full of information and a promise by him that when he was through work he'd drop off, at her hotel, a printout of the capital police summary of all the evidence in the case as well as a photocopy of the CCTV capturing the truck and showing its license plate number.

German proved as good as his word. Irene received the report by late afternoon and spent an early evening, before turning in, reading it. It ran into several pages, included details of the victim's death as listed in coldly impersonal medical terms by the city pathologist—a crushed skull, a number of broken ribs, severe internal injuries, one leg severed from the torso. Death had been instant. Damage to the pickup truck which had hit Judith Freedman amounted to a crushed-in front bumper, crumpled front right fender and right front headlight, as well as both catalytic converter and exhaust pipe torn lose by the victim being extensively dragged under the truck. A sweep of the vehicle had produced no prints. Clearly the person renting it had worn gloves and had rented it with a fake credit card and an assumed name.

"With no motive," the report said, "death was ascertained to be involuntary manslaughter, and one of a half dozen such cases this office investigates every year."

None of it interested Irene. She'd seen such reports a score of times in her career as a police officer, most of them when she was still in uniform. What was of interest, however, was that the truck was a rental. Armed with the name of the renting company and the date of the accident, she left in the morning for the Best Truck Rentals place, across town and conveniently located near the rail station. She wasn't going to take the capital police report as final. She long ago found it best to double-check such reports herself.

Twenty-Six

IRENE FOUND THE BEST Truck Rentals establish-ment was dwarfed into near tucked-away obscurity presence by the better-known car rental offices of Hertz, Avis, Enterprise, and others. In sharp contrast to Andrew German, its sole employee behind a shabby counter was a bearded but weak-looking young man in rolled-up sleeves who clearly resented having to abandon his sandwich lunch and coffee to spend five minutes checking his file for the date of rental on the truck in question after its license number, year, and make were provided for his ease by Irene, who also asked him if he remembered who had rented it.

"We already did all this shit for you fucking cops." Showing resentment in every word, along with a thoroughgoing dislike of the police, the clerk shoved a copy of a rental agreement across the counter at her.

"Well, us fucking cops are doing the same shitty shit all over again, junior," Irene said acidly. "Can you describe the party who rented it?"

"No. Who knows? Some guy. Same as half our clients, gave a fake name and credit card."

"His looks? Tall short? Dark skin, light?"

"Who the fuck could ever remember? Lady,

that hit-and-run was six months ago."

Irene scanned the agreement and took a cell phone photo, hoping the card imprint would show clearly. A little research would reveal criminals who had been known users of fake credit accounts.

"Do you have it out on the lot, or is it being rented at present?"

Taking his time and with body language that spelled resistance at having to do anything, the clerk checked papers on his desk and finally said, "It's out there."

"Where?"

"You have its license number."

Irene had had enough. With one long arm she reached over the counter, grabbed the clerk by his shirt front, and yanked him half over the counter to within inches of her face. "I asked you where in the lot, junior."

A switch clicked in the clerk's sullen resistance. He half twisted around and pointed to a chart of the parking lot. "It's all the way to the back. The far end of the line."

Irene let him fall back into his chair. "When you go home, junior, tell your Mom this shitty cop said she should fucking well teach you manners."

She went out to the parking lot, which she found to be some distance away, as though its presence might contaminate the rows of shiny vehicles belonging to its more important neighbors, and soon found the pickup truck. She was staring at its repaired front end, trying not to picture being struck by it, when she caught movement in the corner of one eye. She turned and saw a boy, high school age, polishing one of the nearby trucks. She said, "Hey there."

The boy saw her. "Ma'am?"

"Spare a moment?"

He came over. "Sure. What do you need?"

Irene showed him her police ID and said, "This truck that killed somebody in a hit-and-run. "Were you working here then?"

"Yes, ma'am. Saw it go out and when they towed it in back in. And oh, boy, what a mess."

"You don't happen to remember whoever took it out?"

"Yeah. Businessman type. Big tall guy in a suit. Didn't look the kind to be renting a pickup."

"Young? Old?"

"Sort of in between. Maybe fifty. Him and the other shorter guy both."

"The other guy?" Irene didn't try to hide her surprise.

"Yeah, there were two of them. Tall older one and a short one. They argued a moment as to who should drive."

"And what did this shorter guy look like? Do you remember?"

"Same. Business suit type. About my height, and he had a beard, sort of, and was getting bald."

"You're sure of that?"

"Yeah. Asked me to run a rag over the headlights, said he would be driving at night."

Irene couldn't remember any second man on the police report she'd received. "Did you tell the cops that?"

"Never saw them. I was off that day when they came."

Irene said, "Would you be willing to sign a statement repeating what you just told me?"

"Sure. Any time. Long as it wouldn't get me in any trouble."

Irene offered a rare smile. "It might get you an official thank you."

She took his name and address, and driving away from the rental lot, she mentally reviewed her next step. It would be visiting the local FBI, where she had a friend with whom she had once worked on a case, to ask for a database search to see if they had any recent baddies who would answer the boy's description of both men.

"One was tall," he'd said, "And had a ponytail but otherwise was a well-dressed typical business-man. The other was short and bald and had a heavy scar running off his nose toward his ear."

That would be all for the moment, but the way things were going, and if her so called "partner" back in Union City had managed to forward the case in no matter how small a way, the FBI was in line to be called in pretty soon, and the whole case taken out of Union City's hands.

Twenty-Seven

CARRIE FELT A LITTLE odd finding herself in charge of an investigation, even if at present it only concerned a missing person. When previously working with the Union City police, she had always been something of a dogsbody and virtually subject to odd orders thrown out by nearly everyone. It had always been, "Hey, kid, I want you to …" But that was then, and this was now.

Finally becoming aware of the role that authority had suddenly thrust on her, she realized it did no good to sit and seethe quietly over Irene Chagas. She had to get to work. And today, not tomorrow. Feeling awkwardly uncomfortable, she called for a general meeting and soon found herself facing the Union City police detective force of six, some far more experienced that herself and assembled before a large board on which were pasted up in pictures and printed notices of progress in a previous crime, a store robbery, that the department was pursuing.

There was Angie Harrow, a wheelchair-bound computer research and CCTV analyst; there was data and research expert Harry Noble, fresh out of uniformed police work and until recently an intern and dogsbody; there was old Herb Kneeter, who, although once effective, no longer was, and should have retired, but stayed on doing clerical work due to Tom Parrier's kindness. Then there was also Mary Rankin, a computer whiz who had proved herself able at hacking; there was Charley Bruzek, who was never called or mentioned by his given name. He had only a plain detective rank but specialized in immediate forensics. And finally there was Salvador Hernandez, who, like Harry Nobel, was only recently arrived from uniformed police work.

There was a moment's expectant silence while they all waited for Carrie to speak and until she got up her courage to do so. When she did, she took a missing persons poster with a large picture of Mary Rose, turned and slapped it onto the board, and said, "We don't know whether Mary Rose is dead or alive. She may very well have been abducted. Or, and it's what we all hope, she may simply have taken off for someplace and didn't want her staff to know.

"Harry, get over to the *Weekly Observer* office, nail everyone working there, and find out if she'd said anything to anybody about being absent, or left a note saying so that might have only just turned up. Nate is the one reporting her missing, so don't listen to any objections from him.

"Angie, check out CCTV at the golf course, and also in town around the newspaper's office. I want to know of any movements by Mary Rose for the past week. Or was there a suspicious appearance of a strange car near hers?

"Herb, check travel agents, please, as well as her bank deposits and withdrawals. If they won't play ball without a warrant, tell Tom. He'll get one fast enough. And Salvador, start asking questions at any place where Mary Rose would likely have done business: her dry cleaner, the liquor store, and whatever supermarket she might have used that's relatively close to her home."

Carrie paused. "But please, everybody, keep a low profile. We don't want universal embarrassment if she turns up sane and sound, which is what we hope for. Nobody's dead until proven so." She paused again, looked around, and then said, "At any time, if you can't reach me and you think you might have run into something important, let Tom know immediately. If there should be serious forensic work involved, he'll want to bring in the CSI unit from their office here."

And then, "Bruzek, you come with me."

"Where to?"

"Mary Rose's home. To see how smart you are."

Bruzek didn't have time to question further. Carrie was out of the room before he could, and he followed, aware for the first time that she was someone who wouldn't brook any hesitance.

She was already behind the wheel of an unmarked police car, its motor started and her seat belt on, when he slipped onto the seat next to her, deciding even as he did to maintain silence, and he stayed that way, as blue-and-red secondary lights flashing from within the rear window of the unmarked car and above the bumper in front, they took off fast for the golf course.

Only minutes later they pulled up in front of Mary Rose's condo, close to the eighth green of the

Brookside Golf Course, the long narrow fairway leading to the green only a few feet away and separated from the condo and the parking area in front of it by a high, almost invisible net fence protecting the condo from mishit golf balls.

Spotting the caretaker two condos back watering down some flower beds, Carrie spoke for the first time. "Bruzek, nail that guy. Get him over here, okay? We need him to let us in. And don't take any shit. He's a prime suspect."

Coming to life and relieved he wasn't having to show his locksmith skills in opening the condo's front door himself, Bruzek quickly rounded up the reluctant janitor and brought him to where Carrie was waiting.

She wasted no time, flashed her badge and said, "Sergeant Driscoll. You'll let me in and then stay right here with Detective Bruzek and answer questions. Any stalling around for whatever reason and I'll have to bring you in for an official interview."

When the caretaker, looking frightened, finally found the right key on his key ring and opened the door, Carrie went inside without another word and, struck at once by the shut-up smell of the place, started a first cursory look around.

She found it all just as Nate Wolkowski had described. There was no sign of a struggle. Car keys occupied the ceramic bowl in the foyer, the nearly empty wine glass stood on the cocktail table before the couch. The television wasn't on, but she remembered Nate saying he'd turned it off.

In the bedroom, the bed had been made but

obviously in haste, and the bathroom showed signs of Mary Rose getting ready for work. There was makeup left scattered about on open shelves, water still puddled in a depression here and there on the floor of the shower, a hair dryer that had not been hung up when used but had been left sitting on the toilet seat.

It would be useless, Carrie thought, for either her or Bruzek to look for fingerprints. Those of any stranger would be lost or half-buried in the avalanche of prints surely left all over the place by Mary Rose. Finger printing would be a job for the CSI guys. And the same went for any DNA, if it turned out it was needed.

Both bedroom and bath, however, produced one shared impression item, Carrie quickly realized. It was the same as was obvious in the living room and kitchenette that she visited in turn where she saw the remains of breakfast that had been dumped in the sink and rinsed but not washed up. The shared conclusion was no sign whatsoever of a struggle. The whole place said in every possible way that Mary Rose had simply upped and walked out after she'd come home at the end of the day.

Back outside, she found Bruzek just finishing up with the caretaker and taking down the man's address and telephone number. "Nothing," Bruzek said when Carrie asked him if he'd picked up on anything. "I think you're probably right," she said, and then to the caretaker, "Okay, you're done here. If we need you again, we know where to find you." She gave the man her card. "And if you hear anything at all, give me a call."

Followed by a silent Bruzek, she went back to the police car and slid in behind the steering wheel. She had just stated the motor when she abruptly turned it off again and sat silently staring into space. She was missing something. She knew she was. What was it?

Twenty-Eight

"WHAT?" BRUZEK FINALLY SAID, when Carrie's silence became deadly and was broken only by the sound of golfers making chips to the green only a short distance away.

"Her car."

Caught short in his own thinking about other things not even remotely connected, it took a moment for Bruzek to connect. "Her car? What about it?"

"We need to check it out."

"Why?"

"Because it figures."

It figures? Bruzek felt stymied. How? It was locked, parked in front of her condo, and the keys for it in a bowl in the foyer of her condo. He started to ask again, then didn't. Something about the way Carrie said it needed to be checked out told him she was onto something. He said a little lamely, "But it's just sitting there, Carrie, with its keys in the bowl in the foyer. She went off without it. Just drove it home and that was that."

"Seems like," Carrie said. "But maybe they drove it."

"They? Who?"

"Remains to be seen. Bring the keys."

Out at the car, and when Bruzek handed her the keys, Carrie opened it up, and pulling a lever near the steering wheel that released the lid of the trunk, said, "I'll take the trunk. You collect any possible scraping of dirt on both the brake pedal, and the accelerator. The driver's floor mat, too, and no matter how small."

She got out from behind the steering wheel. Bruzek thought she'd gone crazy, but he mutely obeyed. He left the car, got out his penknife and a small plastic bag and went to work.

Carrie first opened a back door and carefully looked around. A copy of the *Weekly Observer* lay on the seat undisturbed. "Nothing here," she said to Bruzek, who was kneeling on the ground at the side of the car, his body and head under the steering wheel. She went around to the trunk.

At first sight, Carrie saw nothing. The trunk was empty, nothing apparently out of the ordinary. She bent silently into it, peering everywhere and groping around. *If she'd been dumped in here,* she thought, *there would have to be some sort of a sign. Scuff marks if she was conscious, or if unconscious even blood marks from tied-up ankles or wrists.*

She had almost given up and decided she'd headed down a wrong path when she unexpectedly smelled something vaguely familiar. Bending deeper into the trunk, almost in it herself, she pressed one hand firmly on its carpeted mat to steady herself and then recoiled. Her hand felt vaguely damp. She sniffed her palm and then, straightening, turned to Bruzek, who had come around to join her, and said,

"Guess what? Someone pissed themselves. Mary Rose, right? Who else? It will match up with DNA samples CSI will get off her from all over the place."

Bruzek was suitably impressed. He broke into a grin. "Jesus, you were right," he said, after bending to examine the trunk himself. He held up his little plastic bag. "And I got your dirt samples. Not much but I can probably get more."

Carrie took the plastic bag and looked at the barely visible dirt fallen down into one corner. "Good enough," she said. "Get this to the forensic lab as soon as possible to see if its chemical and mineral properties agree with anything around here someplace. We might come up with a clue as to where she's been taken. It probably can't be all that far."

But although now certain Mary Rose had been abducted, Carrie couldn't find either a clue as to where she was or who the suspects were. She was far from happy, and had the usual sense of failure she always had when an investigation turned up inconclusive.

Visiting her father that evening, in the kitchen of his small sloping-roofed house, she'd brought along a usual pizza and bottle of wine to share, and found Chief Sam Ellis also visiting. Seated with the two elderly men, one still active, the other long retired from police work, she was unable to hide her feelings after she'd explained how far she'd come in investigating the deaths of the Weiss couple in Somersville and now the disappearance of Mary Rose. She said disconsolately, "All that so-called evidence and not a single lead of any kind as to who abducted Mary Rose and who these two killers are."

"Two?" Sam Ellis asked.

"Yes, two. I feel certain there has to be a pair working together, and that they would be the same pair who, if they murdered the Weiss couple, might very well have also murdered Janet Weiss's sister at the capital. Again, I'm sure, but not yet enough evidence to say I have any positive proof. Only that where Janet was concerned, dragging two dead bodies all the way down the lawn to the toolshed would surely have been too much for one person." She shrugged defeatedly.

"Maybe this partner you said you can't stand will come up with some kind of lead," her father offered.

"And maybe not," Carrie said. Something in her bristled at the mere thought of Irene Chagas.

Her father noticed and smiled indulgently. He detected more than disdain for a partner. With Carrie it was never so much the person as the situation, and he detected frustration, which his daughter never had been able to handle well, and deep down that it was the case itself, not the other detective she'd been saddled with.

"Carrie," he said, "you can't win 'em all. You've linked three murders together when nobody else suspected anything—two here, one up at the state capital. And what's more, tied them to a nasty plot to illegally dump waste in the old iron mine with a possible hookup with Washington.

"Finally, you know now Mary Rose isn't just missing. She's been abducted and quite possibly murdered, unless she's being held hostage for some reason. Quite a feat, if you ask me."

"Amen," Sam Ellis said.

Twenty-Nine

WHEN BRUZEK GOT THROUGH talking to Harry Nobel, he looked about for Carrie, and finally found her reporting on their car search to Tom Parrier in his office. "I talked to Harry," he told her when she finally came out. "He got nothing from his visit to the *Weekly Observer*. I mean, nobody there, including Nate Wolkowski, who Harry questioned again, picked up on anything that might give us a lead as to where Mary Rose might have gone."

Carrie's reaction was quick. "As expected," she said, "Okay let's go, then."

"Go where?"

"The *Weekly Observer*."

"But I just said."

"You didn't tell me Harry checked files, Mary Rose's PC and laptop, all that."

Once more accompanying her but feeling a little differently than he had before, Bruzek left the office with her to join her in a police car for the short drive to the *Weekly Observer*. He thought he was beginning to understand why Tom Parrier was so happy to have her back at Union City. She was relentless in her efficiency.

Going directly to Mary Rose's desk after marching through a thoroughly subdued outer office, where at one desk after another its occupant pretended to be studiously at work, Bruzek, without waiting for an order, dove into a PC, the large monitor of which occupied a prominent spot on Mary Rose's desk, along with a mini TV on which the news editor could keep up to date on anything being covered by the local station. While he did, Carrie launched into a methodical search of everything else in the small office.

At first, she found nothing but office memoranda, notes on news items, and drafts of layouts rapidly sketched on foolscap, but finally came onto a file containing paid bills and invoices pertaining to Mary Rose's personal life. Rifling through it, one item suddenly seized her attention. It was a letter, along with an attached invoice from a company announced on the letter head as Your ER Room, under which accompanying script added the words, "no matter where you are." The letter politely stated that Mary Rose was delinquent in paying the previous month's bill and asked her to include payment within thirty days in an enclosed envelope as per the attached invoice.

Carrie waved the invoice and letter. "Bruzek, what the hell is an outfit called Your ER Room?"

Bruzek looked up from staring at the PC monitor, alive with images and print. "It's one of those lifesaving outfits, like you see on TV commercials: 'Help, I've fallen and can't get up.' That sort of thing. Brings out police, firemen, medics."

He'd only half finished speaking when Carrie

started punching in phone number printed at the bottom of the Your ER Room letter. When a voice answered, she said, "Sergeant Driscoll, the Union City Police. I'm looking at a letter from you sent to Mary Rose O'Connell, whose account seems delinquent. I need some immediate information, please."

A surprised woman's voice asked her to hold a moment and almost immediately a more authoritative man came on asking if he could help.

"Yes, please," Carrie said and after identifying herself again, "We need to know if you have recently had any signals from your client, Mary Rose O'Connell."

"Sure. Can you hold a moment?"

She was put on hold again for what seemed forever until the man came back and said, "Mary Rose O'Connell, yes. We have her on record. As you probably know, we cover wherever the client may be, not just their home and home area. Miss O'Connell wears a device as a pendant around her neck rather than attached as a wrist strap, and we received a signal from her only five days ago. Our GPS tracked her as being at a cemetery."

"A cemetery?"

"Yes. We notified you. You should have it on record."

Carrie, surprised, instantly covered. Uniformed police would have received the call but hadn't notified the detective squad. She said abruptly, "We don't have it."

"Oh? That's odd. Well, it was from the Beth Israel Cemetery. In Union City. We picked her up there and were about to send out a general emergency alarm that would have alerted the fire department as well as police and the EMT when the signal stopped. Unusual, since hers was programmed to continue for at least thirty minutes. We telephone her cell phone to see if she'd pressed the device accidentally, but there was no answer, and since we heard no further signals, we presumed it was indeed an error. Just the same, we notified Union City police anyway. Perhaps you'll want to check further."

The first person after Bruzek to hear from Carrie after she had ended the call to Your ER Room was the desk sergeant at police headquarters in Union City, after she and Bruzek returned from the *Weekly Observer* otherwise empty-handed. Bruzek had gone all over Mary Rose's PC for entries during the past three months and had come up with nothing, and she herself had found nothing more to cast light on the news editor's disappearance.

When confronted with a demand as to why he had not registered the call from Your ER Room nor had he reported a subsequent police visit to the cemetery, the desk sergeant, a grizzled veteran, bristled. He had no use for modern police methods or those who practiced it, especially women, even more so a woman with the detective division.

"We sent out a car as requested," He said coldly, "but all the officer ran into was one of those crazy parties the high school kids throw these days. Booze and drugs. Who knows what the kick is they get from rioting in a cemetery? Probably guys getting their rocks off into broads on fallen tombstones."

Carried ignored the vulgarity and his suggestive smirk. "You didn't know the woman was a missing person listing?"

"Missing person? Check your own fucking crowd. Nobody never told us here." The desk sergeant showed his final displeasure of Carrie by dismissively turning his back and talking to a fellow smirking officer.

Carrie snapped back, "Well, I'll let the chief know you've been informed, sergeant. Send us a copy of your officer's report."

Thoroughly annoyed, it was all she could think of to say, and she went back upstairs to the detective offices.

Thirty

"WE LOCK THE GATES at night," the white-bearded old caretaker said, introducing himself as just William after Carrie had roused him from comfortably watching television in the warmth and security of his little cottage by the Beth Israel Cemetery, which was visible through the high heavy iron fence surrounding it. "Doesn't stop the kids, bless the little devils, from getting in anyway. Fences never stopped no one. Can't get over, they go under."

"But what about cars? Don't you lock the gates at night?"

"Lock?" the old man laughed. "One hard rap or two with a hammer on a lock, and in they go. If I've lost one lock in the past ten years, I've lost a dozen. I've given up on locks."

Carrie had driven directly to the cemetery with Bruzek from the police station and now armed with a warrant obtained by Chief Parrier. She didn't say a word of what she had in mind except to express continuing annoyance, even anger, at not being notified of the signal received by the police from Your ER Room.

"What do you expect to find?" Bruzek asked. "Mary Rose lying dead up against some tombstone, or what?"

"Exactly," Carrie said, and Bruzek, deciding it was perhaps better not to question further because he'd find out soon enough, didn't say more.

Walking along a path between rows of headstones and accompanied by William, Carrie asked a question that caught him by surprise. She said, "How many burials have you had these past few days?"

The old man thought a moment or two and then said, "Four. Last one was just yesterday, a dear old lady, used to see her here often laying flowers on her husband's grave. Now she's right next to him."

Carrie said, "I want to see the graves of all four."

William looked at her slightly askance, and seemed poised to ask why, but changed his mind and merely nodded and said, "Whatever suits you, miss."

Bruzek started to ask, "C'mon, Carrie, what this all about?" But again, he didn't. He decided, once again, seeing the set expression on her face, that it would be wise not to, and managed to keep his question to himself.

They reached a first grave, the last resting place of a young man who had been killed recently in some sort of an accident; William couldn't say exactly what or how. The site was a low coffin-length mound of earth that had not sunken down, its rightful space six feet below being taken up by the deceased. It would stay that way for several weeks until some of it settled back into the grave, while any of it that didn't would be carted away, the site raked smooth and planted with grass.

Carrie studied it silently for a moment, then asked to see the next one. It was the grave of a child, and after studying it, she gave it a pass. She gave a pass to the third grave too, but stopped at the fourth longer than at any of the others, and Bruzek noted that the earth mound looked a little dry. It was the grave, William told them, of an elderly woman: "Anna Meister," he said, who had been buried only two days ago next to her husband. "She was a Holocaust survivor who used come and sit a spell by him and then always stop at the cottage and thank me for allowing her to visit."

There was a temporary wooden headstone at the head of the mound, placed there to await a proper headstone. Without really thinking, Bruzek, who had come to stand close to it, reached out, to see if it was securely planted. He was stopped short by a sharp order from Carrie.

"Don't touch that." She got out her cell and punched in numbers. "Tom? Carrie. We've found Mary Rose. We will need CSI forensics and the town medical wagon. Yes, dead. The Beth Israel Cemetery here in Union City." She put away her cell, nodded at the block, and said to Bruzek, who stood back from it, "It could have both prints and DNA on it." And then, to William, "You're about to have a visit from a swarm of cops. Perhaps you'll want to be at the gate to show them where we are."

Bruzek burst out even before she could put away her cell. "Carrie, what the hell?"

Virtually speechless, he could then only stare at Carrie, who smiled back at him and said, "You're wondering where she is? She's right there lying under that mound of dirt, perhaps three feet down. If you look beyond the grave, you'll see a thin line of dirt scattered here and there, some on the pathway between the graves. That's spill from the tarp or blanket or even a plastic sheet her killers used to drag away excess dirt. If it fits the dirt you scraped away from the foot pedals in her car, it means they drove her right up to the cemetery gates."

She turned to an astonished William, who hadn't moved. "Your grave diggers don't leave a trail of dirt behind like that, do they?" She didn't wait for an answer but added, "If we had a shovel with us, we could dig her up immediately. Since we don't, we wait. Bruzek, would you help our friend here back to his cottage?"

Bruzek mutely obeyed. He and William departed, the old man leaning heavily on Bruzek's arm. Reaching the front gates, they didn't have to wait long. Tom Parrier arrived in one of two police cars along with a car bringing three forensic specialists, followed by the coroner's van used to carry bodies definitely pronounced dead.

"So where is she, Carrie?" were Parrier's first words on reaching the gravesite. And when Carrie silently pointed at the mound of fresh dirt, his smile erased. "Wait a minute. Are you're kidding, or what?"

"I'm not."

He stared at her a moment, and then said to one of the white-suited forensic team, "Okay, start digging, and make sure you dust that block of wood for prints, and see if you can wipe DNA from it." He turned to Carrie. "Carrie, I'm banking on your being right. You never told me we'd have to dig her up." His tone was hard and authoritative.

Carrie stayed silent, keeping to herself her wondering what he'd have to say if she proved wrong.

Forensics obeyed, and all that was heard then was the sound of shovels excavating dirt, until the coffin-length pile that had been there had been removed, and with it more fresh dirt from the grave, to a depth of several feet. That's when one of the forensic team said, "Okay, got her."

Five minutes later Carrie and the others surrounding the grave found themselves looking down at the pathetic body of Mary Rose, her wrists plastic-cuffed behind her, her legs also tied together, and duct tape stuck tight across her mouth and eyes. Carrie quickly slipped on gloves and reached down to her, and for Tom Parrier and others to see, held out the small pendant that was suspended from her neck, and said, "Probably got set off when they piled dirt in on her. Smacked by a rock, maybe."

"Understood," Parrier said, staring down at the dead newswoman. "Pathologist should be able to tell us when she died. If how she did is by suffocation, which is my guess, and the time is close to the signal received by Your ER Room, we'll probably learn she was alive when put under. Makes you sick."

Later, and back at the office, as everyone was getting ready to go home, some straight to a nearby bar everyone frequented to get a much-needed drink, Tom Parrier said to Carrie, "One short question, kid. Whatever made you think she was buried there?"

Carrie thought a moment. Why had she? She hadn't known that herself until well after Mary Rose was discovered. She said, "The why? We knew she was in the cemetery from her call to Your ER Room. A fresh-dug and occupied grave could hide forever someone you wanted to get rid of, and her killers figured it an easy and safe place, where there are always fresh-dug graves about. Drop her in, hide her with a two- or three-foot layer of dirt from the fill-in over the recently buried legitimate occupant. Far less work than digging about in a field or the woods someplace, and who would ever suspect burying a body in a grave already occupied? Besides, a cemetery is for burying people, right?"

Thirty-One

IN THE SECOND-FLOOR EXECUTIVE offices in the state capitol building, Lieutenant Governor Jason Hicks, who often worked late, quickly grabbed up some papers he had discarded and laid to one side of his desk, and said sharply, "Hold it."

After dropping the papers hurriedly in the trash bin wheeled past him on a trolley by the night cleaner, he said, "Thank you," and returned to reviewing the memorandum he was to give to the governor as a rough "key points" outline for the governor's talk to the state assembly early in the following week.

Although Hicks hardly noticed, if he did at all, the cleaner was not the same woman who usually did the rounds of the top floor executive offices every night, emptying scrap baskets, sweeping then mopping the highly polished floor, and taking care of the coffee machine, which meant washing the cups left around and refilling the machine with water as well making certain there were enough packets of either coffee or green tea.

It had taken Detective Irene Chagas several days to safely take the place of the regular cleaner who came from an agency that collected a percentage of any cleaner's weekly salary.

The agency, as well as the cleaner herself, had

to be "fixed," and Irene had been too long in the business to feel safe with money bribes. Years of experience had taught her to use something stronger. Granting a momentary pass to the cleaner herself—a woman who, getting along in years, had been working at night cleaning in the capitol building for some time—she decided to aim at the agency head. This was a slightly unsavory woman in her early forties.

First, there'd were hours spent at her laptop looking into whatever she could find about the woman or her husband, an electrical contractor. She was lucky. Both, it turned up, had records: the woman's for relatively minor misdemeanors, unpaid traffic fines, late payments on city taxes, his for a felony. He had done six months for robbery.

Next, she went to work on people connected to the agency head. She questioned the janitor of the apartment building in which the woman and her husband lived, a secretary at the husband's office, a fellow cleaner at the agency. She subdued any revelation of her questioning by whatever minor threat or false promise she could think of that she felt fitted the person.

None of it was anything Irene wasn't skilled at. It was often a relatively standard procedure adopted by many in police detective work to get results when they couldn't be achieved otherwise. Although she told herself, "Get it right, Chagas. Can't shoot yourself out of this one," Irene had been doing the same for years and was good at it. Blackmailing someone to obtain information didn't upset her moral compass. She chalked it up to good police work.

The results she found now were rewarding. The agency head was regularly cheating on her husband, and agreed to anything Irene proposed so as not to be betrayed. That lined her up for a job, and the current cleaner was silenced by a threat to have her blacklisted by the agency head where any other jobs were concerned if she didn't cooperate. That led to her careful instructions of how the job worked, and to join with Irene, carefully dressed and sufficiently bedraggled to pass for the job, in Irene's first two nights to make sure she did everything correctly.

"This is Hilda," the cleaner said with what she'd been coached to say to Jason Hicks and another working late. "She's Latvian or something and doesn't speak much English. Any problems give her a note to take to the agency."

Since the office cleaning never started until eight p.m., Irene was then left to snoop almost as much as she wished. There only remained the two night security guards, and they were both ex-cons who had done varying amounts of time, as so many security guards have. They were directly confronted by Detective Irene and told to cooperate if they wished to keep their jobs. They not only guaranteed silence but instantly set up a system of warning if anyone working on what was called the executive floor unexpectedly came back for some night work.

Wearing a wire, Irene got busy.

In three long nights, once until six in the morning, the top floor offices at the Capitol building were hers, and she all but pillaged not only all the office files of Jason Hicks, the lieutenant governor, but the office of the governor himself. Hicks had never realized, or had cause to, that his password book had been instrumental in Judith Freedman discoveries.

The book was still in the desk drawer where Judith had found it, and Irene now made use of it again to verify what Judith had found and to discover that the book contained not just the password to Hick's computer but the password to the governor's computer, as well as to laptops belonging to two of the governor's staff.

The revelation astonished her. How could anyone involved in such a plot be so careless? But in spite of four tireless nights of examining PCs and laptops, especially the governor's, Irene had just the same come up short on any additional solid evidence. She was still stuck with what Judith Freedman had learned.

She didn't give up, however. Investigating was investigating, whether working on high crimes or minor felonies, and she plodded on. In her experience, luck sometimes showed up when least expected, and this suddenly proved to be true when her investigation was saved by the old-fashioned device of a telephone call, and one made so guilelessly that she was present during it.

She was in Jason Hick's office emptying his and his assistant's scrap baskets and tending, as usual, to the coffee machine, when Hicks pulled his cell phone from his pocket and made a call.

Checking the next day with the telephone

company on the calls Hicks had made from his phone, Irene was told frequent calls had been made to a cell phone listed under the name of Marcus Albright.

Aware, because of Hicks's involvement in the nuclear waste disposal plot, that it could possibly be someone in Washington, Irene, using Hick's PC after he left the office, brought up a database of West Wing employees, and soon found that Marcus Albright was the assistant to the White House Chief of Staff.

She quickly put two and two together, and the following night, while appearing to straighten chairs and begin to sweep up the floor of the day's office debris carelessly thrown there by the office staff, she listened carefully when Hicks was again using his cell phone for a call.

Much of what she heard was the usual one end of a conversation in which the caller at the other end clearly did most of the talking. With Hicks listening, it was "Yes" and "sure," and "No, I didn't," and then "Sure, will do." Irene had almost given up learning anything when she very clearly heard the following brief exchange.

"Who? Arrowsmith? You mean that fucking gunslinger McClellen, right?"

And then, "Yeah, I know, the son of a bitch gets things done. What's his number? I'll give him a call."

Hicks suddenly shot backwards, nearly running into Irene. Still holding the receiver of his phone to his ear, he pointed to trash under his desk and half turned to her. "Get that junk, would you? Thanks."

Irene said, "Yah, yah sir. Sorry, sir," her fake Latvian accent thick. And quickly did as he asked while he continued his talk. "Arrowsmith, sure. Will do, Marcus. Regards to the chief."

Thirty-Two

Marcus Albright had not enjoyed even one minute of the formal state dinner in the White House that was given in honor of the president of the European Union. It was an evening that, as far as he was concerned, was a high-water mark of hypocrisy. Only days ago, the president had denounced the European Union as useless, as well as its president, Dag Bjorkwold. The Danish notable had flown in only the day before from Copenhagen to be greeted with all possible official protocol followed today by Rose Garden speeches from both men along with their much publicized shaking of hands.

Marcus, in fact, had barely noticed the presence of his wife seated in her new thousand-dollar Givenchy evening dress next to him at the table set in the crowded room for eight privileged officials of the White House inner circle. She was positively glowing at having finally achieved what was for her the height of social success she had for so long only dreamed of. Nor was Marcus but only slightly aware of the riotous performance of a celebrity comedian who satirized US-EU relationships, or the famed gospel chorus brought in from St. Louis, or the brief segment of *Swan Lake* provided for the entertainment by the New York City Ballet.

All that had mattered to Marcus was the new newspaper clipping from the Union City *Weekly Observer.* It had occupied every moment of his thinking before and during the dinner since he'd retrieved it in its anonymous envelope from his mailbox when he arrived at his suburban home in Bethesda after he'd rushed home from work at the White House to get ready for the evening.

Now, twenty-four hours later and again arriving home, he parked his car in the expansive three-car garage and went up the short flagstone walk to the front door. Entering, he heard his wife call out, "Marcus?" Responding that he'd be with her shortly, he went to his study, locked the door behind him, and plunked down into his desk chair. Hurriedly removing the offending news clipping from a desk drawer where he'd kept it secret all day, he spread it out carefully on his blotter. Bylined by Nate Wolkowski, it was headlined in bold letters, "*Weekly Observer*'s Editor Slain," and Marcus read it again perhaps for the fifth time.

Mary Rose O'Connell, editor in chief of the *Weekly Observer,* who had been missing for several days, was found dead today in the Beth Israel Cemetery after an extensive search led by Sergeant Driscoll of the Union City Police.

The bound and gagged body of the newswoman was found buried in the upper part of a grave in which there had been a previous interment of octogenarian Anna Meister only twenty-four hours before. "Mary Rose was buried alive," Chief of Police Tom Parrier declared, and he vowed that the full force of the Union City Police, assisted by a special unit of the state police, would be employed to run down the killers in this most brutal and heinous crime on state record.

Marcus turned away from reading. There was more, a lot more: a virtual biography of Mary Rose O'Connell's life and speculation as to the motive behind the murder, followed by a paragraph about the danger to freedom of the press, something Mary Rose had been a staunch defender of.

Marcus thought carefully. He hadn't shown General Lansdowne the letter. Bringing the general into it opened the chance that the general, always seeking to avoid anything at all costs that might reflect on himself, could find a way to turn it back on him as a scapegoat. In the West Wing you soon learned not to risk the wrath of anyone superior to you, whether you were guilty of something or not.

After another moment's careful thought, Marcus extracted his cell phone from a side pocket of his jacket, hesitated again, then punched in a number that belonged to a well-known chiropractor. The phone rang three times and was answered by a female voice, "Dr. Hooker's office."

Marcus said, "Marcus Albright. Ask Doctor Hooker to call me," and abruptly hung up and waited, secure in the knowledge that he'd never hear from Dr. Hooker. His request would be immediately transferred on her personal cell phone by his receptionist, who earned a welcomed bonus from Marcus for forwarding such calls to McClellen at Arrowsmith, then deleting she had ever made them.

Marcus didn't have to wait long. A familiar

number flashed on his cell phone's display, and before he could even say his name, McClellen's voice said, "I've already read it, Marcus. What do you want done?"

Marcus said, "How far up the line do you think this looking for the woman's killers could go?"

"Nowhere you need to worry about," was the answer, "unless they tie into the ones in Somersville and the state capital."

"And then?"

"Then they will most likely bring in the FBI."

"Do you seriously think there's a chance of that?"

"Possibly yes, possibly no."

"Possibly? Fuck possibly, McClellen. Which is it?"

There was a long silence, too long for Marcus. "McClellen?"

An answer finally came. "Yes or no? It's probably up to the detectives on the case. To ring in the FBI, they would have to decide whether or not they have credibly linked all the crimes mentioned."

That was enough for Marcus. He said bluntly. "Be sure you know whether they keep it local or don't, McClellen."

And without another word, Marcus turned off his phone and deleted the call he had received.

Thirty-Three

IT WAS ONLY THREE days after her evening with the two old veterans of police work that Carrie found herself in Tom Parrier's office, meeting with Irene, back from her work in the far-off state capital. She tried to listen civilly to the woman's report, and when it came to her own work, she summarized it, only briefly touching on Mary Rose's murder while bearing with Irene's dismissal of it as unimportant.

"Interesting locally," the older detective said, but I don't see any proof of its connection to the two sisters, one down here, one up at state."

To further throw cold water on Carrie's discovery of Mary Rose's body, she added, "Has any further work been done on their case, or am I the only one getting on with it?"

Carrie bristled. "Mary Rose was writing about the twin sisters' deaths," she said. "That in itself links her to them."

"Your hunch or a hypothesis, sergeant?" Irene countered and with a dismissive air that bordered on boredom. "Whichever, it stops right there. Successful investigations aren't based on either. Tell me when you have something solid to seriously link to your newspaper editor."

Carrie was glad Parrier was present, and from

the start had let him do most of the talking, which, for the most part, were only questions about Irene's role in the case. Answering Parrier's about the phone talk she'd overheard, Irene explained Arrowsmith. "It's well-known internationally for providing soldiers of fortune to countries in an uproar and wanting more firepower for some more killing. The horror who runs it is a mug named McClellen with a record a mile long of his own that's never been pinned on him to send him away for life. The lieutenant governor was talking about him to some guy in the West Wing.

"Interesting," she continued, "but meaningless if we can't tie it in to specifics. For a start, that meant having a look at the killer truck, so I followed up on the parking lot boy's revelation of two men renting it the day of Judith Freedman's death, and then paid a visit to the local FBI and talked an old friend into letting me have an ex officio look at their database of known hit men.

"I pulled up a score of photos of likely suspects," she said. "Two seemed more likely than any others, so I copied and took their shots back to the truck rental lot and showed them to the kid. He identified them immediately. So now we not only have verification that there were two killers but who they are. They both have histories linking them to unsolved murders. One is a psychopath, plain and simple, the other originally from some country in the Middle East where he was a notorious prison guard responsible for endless torture deaths. The FBI has DNA on one of them. Nice, yes. But with no DNA down here to match it with, where does it get us?"

When the meeting drew to a close, with Parrier admonishing Carrie and Irene to keep at it, he added, "Carrie, nobody's perfect. If you're right about Mary Rose being connected to your two sisters' murders, then these guys Irene's uncovered could be Mary Rose's killer too. If so, they would have had to have left some evidence behind somehow and somewhere, maybe linking them up. Your cookie. Do your best."

Like I hadn't already, Carrie thought bitterly when back at her desk. But where to begin? Other than the Your ER Room lead, she had nothing further, no prints, no DNA. She'd found nothing on Mary Rose's computers, nor letters, nor anything on any of the files in the office that might definitely tie Mary Rose to the same pair who had killed the Weiss couple and Judith Freedman. All she had was that the newspaper editor's body had been carried in her own car and the two news columns she'd written about the murders of Judith and Janet. Neither got her anywhere.

Even more despairing was noted in Carrie's two-word question to Bruzek a day later. "Any ideas?" She had thought that the two killers might have stopped off for something to eat while possibly conning the newspaper's offices when planning their kill, perhaps even stayed at the local hotel. She and Bruzek had questioned employees and searched several of Union City's more popular lunch counters in the vain hope that if either killer had eaten there, he might have left his DNA on a cup or utensil or a plate that hadn't yet been washed. The result? No evidence of any kind found, let alone DNA.

"The gents?" Bruzek had suggested. "A flush handle on a urinal?"

"Like nobody pissed in the same urinal since?" Carrie said. Her sarcastic dismissal put an end to any further search in lunch counters.

"We're chasing bloody rainbows," Bruzek grumbled morosely. "The bastards were born with gloves on. Latex surgical ones at that most likely." Forensics had reported finding nothing from a woolen glove, a speck of lint or wool fragment. Nor any indication the gloves they wore were leather, which would have left a near invisible image detectable only through an electron microscope.

The picture in her mind of someone pulling on surgical gloves, not to heal as doctors and nurses always did but to kill, sickened Carrie. And it was the kind of haunting picture that, like an old melody, simply refused to go away. No matter how hard she tried to make it do so, it kept coming back, over and over again, all the rest of the day and back again that night.

After a bad night's sleep, she was making first-in-the-day coffee for herself and Terry when she spilled some on the table. She rushed and got some paper toweling to mop it up when Terry intervened and took the sodden toweling from her. "I'll take care of it," he said, and dumped the sodden mess into the garbage pail under the sink.

Something in his doing so jarred Carrie. When Terry came back to the table and sat down again, he saw her staring blankly off at nothing.

"What's wrong?"

"Nothing." But then, "Terry, don't doctors and nurses always take off their latex gloves when they're through examining? And throw them out?"

"Yeah, I guess. What got you onto that?"

Carrie managed a smile and hid behind her coffee mug. "Just being me." She thought that if she allowed herself to think one more minute about latex gloves, she'd lose her mind. Making an effort, she quickly changed the subject, asking Terry his plans for the day, and while pouring more coffee, submitted to his outlining his idea for a meeting that afternoon at the Old Mill with its owners to discuss his plans for it.

Thirty-Four

CARRIE'S RELIEF FROM THE disturbing imagery didn't last long. Once back in the police office and pretending to work on a summary of the case so far, the picture of someone pulling off latex gloves kept coming back and back until it became the anonymous figure of one of Mary Rose's killers standing over her freshly covered grave and, his ghastly work done, putting down his shovel and pulling off his latex gloves.

The picture stayed, and then suddenly exploded in Carrie's mind, and she pushed back her chair and stood up. Fast. "Bruzek?"

The sharpness in her voice startled the detective, who, two desks away, was half asleep, staring at his computer screen and the data figures on various hit men that he'd scrolled down. He found Carrie next to him, shrugging into her jacket, her holstered Glock already strapped on at her waist.

"Let's go," she ordered.

"Go? Go where?"

She didn't answer, and she was halfway to the door when Bruzek, who knew better than to argue with her, reluctantly scrambled to his feet and followed.

Carrie helped herself to a parked idle police car,

and the moment Bruzek managed to pile in beside her, she accelerated off, roof lights flashing, before he could even get his seat belt on.

"Jesus, Carrie. Could you at least slow down long enough to give me an idea?"

"The Beth Israel Cemetery."

"The cemetery?"

There was no answer, and as they hurtled through traffic and out into the suburbs, Bruzek didn't say a lot of things he wanted to say. He wanted to protest, "What the hell?" and "The fucking cemetery? Are you kidding me?" But he was getting to know his superior detective better and better, and maintained a guarded silence. Whatever it was she had in mind, it would come out sooner or later.

At the cemetery's big iron gates, securely shut with a chain and a padlock, the elderly white-haired William didn't try to hide his surprise at the sudden arrival of the police car. When its motor died along with its flashing red-and-blue roof lights, and the two cops he at once recognized stepped out, he could only manage two words. "What now?"

Carrie said, "Back to the grave site. I'll need you to come."

For a moment the old man stared at Carrie, then took in the police car and realized that protest was useless. His mind on the cup of tea he'd just made for himself, which would now get cold, he reluctantly got his jacket from inside his gate house along with a key ring.

"Keep the place locked up now," he said. "Kids."

And removed the chain that barred the entrance. Once Carrie and Bruzek were through, he led them along the paved path only just wide enough for a hearse as it wound its way amidst scores of graves, a few new but mostly old, their headstones remembering lives once lived, until it reached the one where they had discovered Mary Rose buried several feet under and just above the elderly Anna Meister.

Carrie wasted no time pointing out to Bruzek the trickle of dirt she'd seen before. "See that? It spilled from a blanket or a plastic sheet, remember? We got a match for it from her car. When they took away extra dirt, they didn't use to make the grave look as untouched as it was before." Without expecting an answer or waiting for one, she turned to the old caretaker. "Where did they take it? The extra dirt?"

William looked momentarily as puzzled as Bruzek at the question and then he said, "The dirt? Well, I guess that would have to be the dump."

"Okay, where's that?" The old man pointed vaguely, and Carrie added, "You'll have to show us the way."

William shrugged his thin shoulders and started off slowly. Carrie and Bruzek followed silently until, ignoring the questioning looks Bruzek threw at her, Carrie took heart at the caretaker's almost faltering steps and ordered Bruzek to "Run and get the car so we can ride our friend back to the gate house. And bring a shovel if you can find one."

When the ever-wondering Bruzek reluctantly obeyed, she continued to follow the old man's faltering steps, and soon found herself at the very edge of the cemetery, in an area where graves had not yet been dug and where right by the iron fence surrounding the entire cemetery there was a large pile of dirt and rubble. Parked by it was the backhoe used to dig graves and a small golf cart–sized truck used to carry dirt that could navigate the gravel paths between the graves. At one side of the pile, the one closest to the narrow paved road, there was a smaller one of dirt that seemed relatively fresh.

Won't need the shovel after all, Carrie thought. *Not that much.* Trying not to think of the newspaper editor she was certain it had been removed to accommodate, she went right to the dirt pile, and kneeling down, began to dig around with her bare hands. It took longer than she thought, and she had only got to what she searched for when Bruzek came up from the gates and their parked police car.

She stood and held up the latex glove she retrieved d from the dirt and laughed and said, "The DNA we need."

Thirty-Five

N ATE WOLKOWSKI, NECKTIE REMOVED and his collar unbuttoned, sat at the desk usually occupied by Mary Rose and looked with a kind of deep satisfaction at the front page article under his byline in the *Weekly Observer*, the publication of which he had supervised as the paper's new editor.

Following a headline that boldly declared "Nuclear Waste Disposal Plot Uncovered," the article filled two columns and read:

Local detectives of the Union City force under Police Chief Tom Parrier, and joined by Somersville's Sergeant Cassandra Driscoll, have uncovered a Washington plot to illegally dispose waste from the defunct Orion nuclear power plant. The plot is now believed to possibly reach as high as the West Wing.

The discovery, currently in the hands of the FBI, came as the result of an investigation into the shocking death of Mary Rose O'Connell, the longtime editor of this newspaper. First reported missing, her tortured body was discovered by detectives only this past week in the Beth Israel Cemetery, where she was buried alive.

Revelation of the newspaper editor's brutal murder followed an investigation lasting some months into the murders last spring of both Judith Freedman at the state capital and the double murders, first thought to be suicides, of her sister, Janet Weiss, and her husband, Sidney Weiss, a retired cartographer, both longtime residents of Somersville.

A twin sister to Janet, Judith Freedman, was an assistant in the office of Lieutenant Governor Jason Hicks. According to confidential sources, discovery by Judith of our state's corrupted legislature's involvement in the illegal waste disposal was aided by our governor as well as by Mr. Hicks. This was revealed, this newspaper further learned, when assembly leader Tony Mellor, apparently under pressure from Washington, reversed himself and forced a legislature vote that allowed Guthrie to begin to prepare the old iron mine.

We have further learned that this led to an alarmed exchange of texting and emails between the two sisters, which were uncovered by Detective Sgt Driscoll. These exchanges, along with both computers used for their transmission, are now in the hands of authorities.

It's believed there were two murderers of Mary Rose O'Connell. A DNA sample left by one of them has led to the connection between her death and the murders of the Weiss couple and Judith Freedman. A resulting nationwide alert has been issued for two notorious hit men disguised as presentable businessmen and believed responsible for the past murders of over a dozen people. They are presumed armed and dangerous. A news blackout has now been imposed on all branches of the media.

Nate tipped back in his chair and enjoyed a deep satisfaction that seemed to magically flow through every corner of his body. Even if he said so himself, he was impressed. A front-page byline and editor of the paper as well? Besides the glory of his article, there was his relief of being out from under the too often dictatorial weight of Mary Rose, who never seemed satisfied with anything he did or wrote. Many were the times when after being berated by her for one minor offense or another, he impulsively had decided to quit and work elsewhere. Where that would be with the *Weekly Observer* the only newspaper in Union City was the question, however, and one that stopped him from acting on it every time. Now he was able to bathe in the satisfaction of having held his tongue.

In the Union City police offices, Carrie at first felt a similar satisfaction over the news article. Not over the article itself, but over having been the one to come up with the DNA taken from the interior of the latex glove worn by Mary Rose's killer and which had irrevocably linked all four murders together. That had been her part in presenting a case that both police chiefs, Tom Parrier at Union City and old Sam Ellis at Somersville, felt obliged to take to the FBI.

Grudgingly, she had to admit to herself, but to nobody else, that it had taken two to tango. Her despised partner, Irene Chagas, had, after all, come up with the identities of the murderers of three women and a man and even the names under which they were listed on the FBI's most wanted list. Besides this, she had ferreted out a clandestine organization, Arrowsmith, heavily involved with all four murders and with ties to the White House.

Acknowledgment didn't lessen, however, having to stand smilingly close to Irene while both received equal praise for their "stellar police work in bringing to light a major crime of danger to the whole nation," when present at the clamorous televised press conference that was presided over by the state's attorney general, along with Union City's mayor and district attorney, as well as chiefs Ellis and Tom Parrier.

While euphoric, Carrie was also subdued. With the intensity of the case gone, she felt strangely let down, out of sorts. Now what? While there was slightly more crime in Union City than in the near crimeless Somersville, there was, just the same, little for a detective to do out of the utterly mundane: a stolen car, a neighborly dispute, marital or sexual abuse, a bar fight or the occasional shoplifting, and the boring job of school guarding.

So she felt almost the opposite of Nate Wolkowski. Where he was only too happy that he could now stay put, Carrie was miserable at the thought that there was no true crime for her to go after, making whether she was unhappy or not irrelevant.

The aloof superior air continuously adopted by Irene Chagas, with whom she'd been forcibly partnered by Chief Parrier, didn't help. Once she'd made her own report on what she'd achieved at the state capital, Chagas had only recognized Carrie's outstanding work in recovering the DNA-bearing latex glove with a nod and the briefest of remarks, "Good thing you did," which in its very context implied a discipline-worthy failure if she hadn't.

The only thing that for Carrie took some of the depressing sting out of Chagas was Terry, who was visibly overwhelmed with admiration for her—"I finally found out what you do. You're great, gal. Just great."

He dropped always enthusing about his own

work and ambitions, which he blamed on her never talking about her own. "I wish you'd tell Chagas what you tell me," she said, when, to celebrate seeing her on television, he took her to a candlelit dinner that to Carrie was sheer heaven.

Her father had much the same to say. "Carrie, for you the case was all important," he said, when feeling guilty at having neglected him for several days, she showed up of an evening with the inevitable pizza and bottle of wine, and at one point launched a verbal attack on Irene. "For her, from all you tell me, it was probably not that important, but probably just another case. How long has she been a cop? Thirty years? Thirty-five? She must have worked a dozen relatively big ones just in her previous job, while you, even though in that one shoot-out, have really only worked on this one."

"She's a bitch."

Her father had laughed. "Perhaps. Haven't met the lady. But did it ever occur to you that all her standoffishness and putting on superior airs might be a sign of just plain boredom? Or even loneliness? The way you described her to me, like her being a getting-old-too-soon underfed horse, could indicate that. Is she married? No? Boyfriend? A no there also?"

Carrie had left her father's concern unanswered. She dismissed loneliness or the boredom he'd offered for Irene's coldness when he'd said, "Or, ever thought she might just be burned out and totally fed up with police work?"

"Nobody's forcing her to be a cop."

"Oh, come on, Carrie. Be fair. What else is she going to do at her age?"

"Go to work for the Post Office. You did."

"Possibly. Yeah." George Driscoll had sighed and hadn't pursued any support of Irene Chagas further.

But things he'd said rang a distant bell somewhere deep within Carrie. He'd planted a thought and it nagged when she'd returned to the police station in Union City and found herself again sitting near a mostly silent partner and having to talk to her about a new case involving bank fraud that had cropped up suddenly and to which they had both been assigned.

Thirty-Six

WHERE THE NEW INFORMATION came from, Marcus Albright didn't know, and he realized that he never would. People in Washington who blew whistles found it an easy swamp to hide in. He could guess, though, and he guessed it was again a reporter, this time probably someone at National Cable News seeking as usual to curry favor with the president, while at the same time fortifying the extremist elements who were behind most of the false facts the TV cable station disseminated nationwide as well as endlessly to the president himself.

Getting home, he rushed into the refuge of a shower in hope that the warm water enveloping his head and shoulders would somehow provide safety from further Oval Office presidential fury. The news had got to the president, and they'd been summarily summoned to the Oval Office, then whipped by the full seething anger of the president's famous silent, tight-lipped disapproval for nearly two hours.

With neither he nor General Lansdowne able to adequately concoct a defense, they eventually learned that the president had been informed of the press conference at faraway Union City and when, during it, a nuclear waste disposal plot was revealed that involved some of his most ardent political allies, including Tony Mellor, the notoriously corrupt leader of the state legislature, and even the governor himself.

"How was this allowed to happen?" the president had hissed, his graying face growing even grayer. He had stopped his tongue-lashing only long enough to grab up a telephone and demand to be put through to the attorney general himself. "If that useless simpering fool can't have the FBI stifle this, I'll have his head on a block." Then, waiting for the call to be placed, he had directed his wrath at Lansdowne. "And you with him, General Lansdowne. Don't tell me you didn't know about this."

"Sir …"

"Shut up. Speak when asked to. And don't tell me you didn't know. You're the guy in charge."

That was only the start. It had gone on for more than an hour while he and Lansdowne sat in silence, trying to piece together what had happened, and as terrified for their own welfare, as full details of the press conference slowly emerged, as they were of the president.

"Get hold of Arrowsmith," a grim-faced Lansdowne had said the moment they were released by the president with orders to "Bury this mess, or else. And I don't mean next week."

They were the only words Lansdowne spoke before the general shut himself in his office. As shaken as the Chief of Staff, Marcus had got through to McClellen and arranged an urgent meeting.

"My place," he said, when McClellen had come on the line and he'd explained what had happened. "And tonight."

Hanging up, he silently thanked the gods that his wife was away for several days visiting her mother in Connecticut. An hour later, he opened the front door to McClellen and ushered him into his study, locking the door behind him and not bothering with preliminaries. Although he'd only mentioned the barest details over the phone, he was certain McClellen had already thoroughly briefed himself.

"These bastards of yours aren't supposed to fuck up, and they did." He threw the accusation at McClellen almost before the man had sat down.

McClellen came right back at him. "One in several millions," he snapped. "They hardly expected to run into a psychic bloody cop."

"Well, they damn well did. And besides leaving a latex glove around, where else did they screw us?"

"Nowhere else."

"I'll believe that," Marcus said, "when nothing else shows up."

"Don't hold your breath, Albright," McClellen threw back. "And I didn't come here to listen to you complain. Leaving a latex glove in a dirt pile in a cemetery is going to cost me shipping my boys out, off to a safe country, and when there, into a safe house. You guys want to foot the bill for that?" When Albright didn't answer, McClellen laughed. "I thought not. Now calm down tell me what you know about what the FBI has been handed, and

I'll tell you what I know, okay?"

Marcus stared at the weak-looking pallid man lounging in a chair as though he owned the place and tried to curb the rising venom he felt. If he didn't go to the West Wing tomorrow with some specifics for Lansdowne, he would almost certainly be out of a job. Anything he said was saving himself, even if he had to exaggerate the homework he'd done in the several phone calls to political allies around Washington that he'd made immediately after the meeting with the president.

What was clear was that McClellen's two hit men had turned in the kind of professional job they'd been asked to do and paid for. The clueless murder of Judith Freedman at the state's capitol and the murder of Janet Weiss had been linked but only circumstantially. Work by one of the two detectives on the case at the state capital had identified the two killers, and work by the cop in Union City who had started the investigation by disbelieving a suicide had been equally useless until the Union City cop had linked all four murders together.

Thinking it all out before McClellen's arrival, Marcus had silently cursed. McClellen was right. A carefully engineered scheme for the president to profit from a state's corruption in disposing of atomic waste had been thwarted by plain bad luck—the discovery of a thrown-away latex glove on a cemetery dump pile. Nothing else.

"McClellen listened carefully to everything Marcus said, then added what he knew of the complexity of steps already taken in the state's capital to make any participation or interest by the president remained unknown.

"It's mostly a question of debts being paid or coming home to rest," he explained. "State politics can be a nightmare of chicanery, and what has often gone on in the state in question is no exception. For a start, the governor owes a big one to the state's legislative leader, who, in exchange for political favors, has held back from revealing the governor's carefully buried assistance in stifling the investigation into the voting fraud of a few years ago.

"Damage control? It will be up to you guys to engineer it politically, which I'm sure the president can do. He has the AG in his pocket, and the AG will jump when told to, so the FBI will get nowhere on this one. Unless, of course, this out-of-control little cop down in Union City gets some new idea for a scandal in her head or gets big-headed and dines out on this one too often for her own good. I'll see my boys take care of her before they skip country."

Thirty-Seven

WHEN HER ALARM WENT off at six thirty, Irene roused herself wearily. Getting out of her narrow sofa bed and going to work was becoming harder and harder as each day passed. She felt as though every bone and fiber in her body was saying, "No, don't move. Sleep." But no such luck. She made it to the bathroom, took a shower, and in the small bed alcove of her studio apartment selected clean pants and a shirt from the relatively meagre supply hanging in her only closet. Dressed, she went to the kitchen section of the room and made herself coffee.

Taking it to the worn easy chair where it sat before a low wooden table, she remote-flicked on the television and tried to face going to work. The mere thought of it was depressing. Today was yet one more working day in a parade of them that stretched so far back into the past that she, for the life of her, couldn't remember why she had first started in the business of being a cop. Had she felt the job might be glamorous or something? Probably. But now, one more day of meaningless work and two more years of "one more days" and she'd be forced to retire, but with a pension, and thank God for that.

But then what? Retire, yes, but retire where, and to do what? She had a cousin on the coast, she remembered, but she was long married and she'd hardly want to welcome an aging single woman she hadn't seen in twenty years who was seeking advice or help in getting started with a new life so completely unconnected with the old. There'd been one or two colleagues at her previous job, but you couldn't go back. A good-bye to a coworker meant just that—good-bye, and she couldn't go back there for any other reason anyway. There'd been too much bad feeling between her and the chief and the district attorney when she'd refused to bear witness against a young man charged in a homicide while part of a ring of auto thieves. She had thought that evidence showed him innocent.

She tried to imagine herself living outside of a city but someplace not too isolated from supermarkets and the occasional movie. Florida, maybe? Theoretically it was warm there most of the year. But where in Florida? The thought of one of those retirement communities, scores of the rapidly getting old, many widows or widowers, all thrown together with nothing in common and all pretending how great life was as they also pretended, or tried to, like one another. That was out as far as she was concerned. Was there anybody else? Or any other place? She didn't think so.

After a while, the coffee took hold. She pulled herself together, securely strapped on her holster with its Beretta handgun, threw on her denim jacket, and taking a deep breath, left her apartment.

It was on a busy block, and walking to the police station some twenty minutes away, she began thinking about the immediate work ahead. With the uproar wrapping up the last case over, what would Chief Parrier have on the plate to investigate? Probably not much. And perhaps not even enough to dump most of it on her so-called "partner" who had received so many kudos for her DNA linking the murder of the newspaper woman to the three others.

Typical, Irene thought, that a relatively small-town novice should reap the glory while the work done by a longtime veteran like herself was usually taken for granted. So, okay, Driscoll had been decorated for her part in the shoot-out some months back; she had guts, no doubt of it, but that wasn't detective work. And she was a nice kid too. It was hard not to like her a little. But being nice got you nowhere as a cop.

She was still vaguely wondering what the day would hold when she found herself in the already busy police office and dropping into a seat before her assigned desk on which she was surprised to find a Dunkin coffee container. She was wondering why it was there, who had left it, when she heard Carrie from her own desk a few feet away, "Thought you might want one. So when I bought mine I got an extra."

Irene pushed the coffee to one side and said, "I already had one," and at once busied herself at her computer. But at the same time almost immediately asked herself why she hadn't at least said, "Thanks."

The girl was obviously trying to be friendly. That was okay, except she didn't want her to be. Being friendly meant the person befriended had to be friendly back, and Irene had along since learned that at work friendships or any attempt at them never added up. They meant a relationship, and relationships got in the way of the clear thinking that most detective work required to be successful.

A call from Parrier stopped any further thought. Irene reluctantly gathered her notepad and joined Carrie to hear what he had in mind.

"A YouTube case," Parrier began. "Teenagers. Got a call this morning from a frantic mother," he glanced at his notepad, "a Mrs. Ann Richardson. Something about a video of her fourteen-year-old daughter Michelle posted on YouTube. Number 27 Chelsea Street. It's a private home. Run over and see what's going on. And if it's bad, like the daughter posing in the naughty or blowing some dude, or the centerpiece in a threesome, find out who's behind the posting."

As she and Carrie rose to leave, Irene thought, *Here it goes once more. Another day of other people's lives.*

Thirty-Eight

D RIVING TO 27 CHELSEA Street, Carrie, behind the wheel, was as silent as Irene, but her thoughts weren't. She felt a little miffed at the way the lanky horse-faced woman had dismissed the coffee she'd brought up to her as a sort of make-peace gesture. After the talk with her father, she'd begun to think that she was perhaps being a little intolerant. Maybe there was something nice about Irene that wasn't on the surface, or perhaps there were some sort of hidden problems that were souring her.

Remembering that Irene was a cop heading toward retirement, she wondered what she had planned. There hadn't been any evidence in the months Irene had been with the Union City police force that she had a family or children, and apparently she had little social life. Had all the years of ardent and intensive police work made any of that impossible? And would she end up the same, Carrie wondered, realizing even as she did that except for Terry, she had no social life at all, other than him, and as for family, her father wasn't going to last forever. When he was gone, her family was zero.

Oh, stop being negative, Carrie, she told herself. But the admonishment didn't help much because once at 27 Chelsea Street and listening patiently to Ann Richardson's near hysterical complaints about her daughter Michelle's waywardness, she found herself drawn right back into looking over her own life.

Ann Richardson might complain; her complaints might even be valid. Michelle might be an oversexed teenaged fool persuaded through drugs to pose naked for porn pictures, but at least Ann Richardson had a life. She had a husband and a child; she had still-living parents. And part of her hysteria was what her wide circle of friends would think of her because of her daughter's behavior. Could a Sergeant Cassandra Driscoll match any of that?

When Carrie and Irene Chagas finally left a slightly calmed mother and a sobbing daughter with promises to bring to justice the culprit who was behind launching the video out over cyberspace, with all its thousands of viewers, Carrie had begun to think that the only way she could not end up like her detective partner would be to start right now taking a serious interest in Terry and his life, not just her own. How about, for a start, his project of converting the Old Mill into condos, which so often had unjustifiably bored her. If a success, it could lead more rapidly to his becoming a congressman and possibly their both moving to Washington because of it.

Once the thought seized her, Carrie decided to act. She'd start tomorrow, she thought, as they pulled up at the police station and went inside.

Once in the office they were barely at their desks when Parrier emerged from his office, a sheaf of papers in his hand, including a copy of the *Weekly Observer*. "Got the bloody press on our backs," he said. "Nate Wolkowski. Just got a call from him. He wants to know all the dirty details."

"About the Richardson video?" Irene muttered. "Jesus. The jackass. Nothing better to write about? Okay, no sweat. We'll get busy on it."

She flicked on her computer and said to Carrie, "Get a list of all the stupid kid's classmates at school, boys and girls. We'll start from there."

It wasn't a suggestion; it was an order, and Carrie bristled. She said, "You plan to interview all of them? Can't we weed out the impossibles first? Like Michelle's closest friends?"

"Each and every," Irene replied. "At their homes, preferably where any lying will be more obvious. Kids lose their cool in front of their parents." She laughed. "Quite a comedown from latex gloves, right? And while we're at your past glory, you'd better watch yourself. You're probably still a problem to whomever."

Carrie felt a sudden chill, and then dismissed it, as she had done with remembering almost all the details of Mary Rose's horrible end. Irene had turned her back and was busy writing something. Around her the office hummed. Carrie rose. "I'm off to high school," she said, as she slung her handbag over one shoulder. Without waiting for a reply from Irene, although she doubted there would be one, she headed for the door.

Irene, bent on tracing the video of the Richardson child performing sexually, got the name and a number of a video camera supplier from her computer and rose in turn. *Waste of time,* she thought, *to try to get an answer via computer. Best to tackle whomever personally.*

Irene was not one to waste time once her mind was made up. Minutes later she was downstairs, headed for a car and just in time to see Carrie, who had paused to chat with a couple of uniformed cops, get into an unmarked car the detectives used and drive away.

"Damn," Irene said aloud. "A moment sooner and I could have had a ride." She checked again the address she'd written in her notebook. It wasn't far, and she set off to walk it.

Thirty-Nine

FRANCES ASTER, THE HIGH school principal, and even though still young, had about her the same dreariness as the building in which she supervised the education of several hundred children and which, in trying to look classic in its architecture, seemed tired with age and out of keeping with the modern life that swirled through the street it was on.

Seated behind her office desk, which had always served as a protective fortress against unwanted problems or responsibilities, Frances had found herself reluctantly facing, through her large horn-rimmed glasses, someone who was implacably unresponsive to whatever objections she raised. For ten minutes and instead of answers or arguments, or hopefully even agreements, she had received only a level, cold-eyed, and silent stare from the young police officer who'd been announced as Sergeant Driscoll.

"So, precisely, sergeant," she asked, "what do you suggest I do? Once again, and please try to understand. I give you a list of names, and before you've interviewed three of them, I'll have all three hundred and sixty-five parents, to say nothing of their kids, down on my neck demanding to know why I've given them out. To say nothing of having an irate school superintendent demanding the same."

The rise in Aster's voice, normally measured, calm, and always authoritative when she spoke, was a clear indication of irritation and defeat in the primly officious woman, usually steely and unforgiving, especially where students were concerned.

Carrie realized that she was going to have to use heavy leverage, something she always left as a last resort. "Mrs. Aster," she said in a quiet voice, "you have a choice. You give me a list of every child in Michelle Richardson's class, and right now, or I will have to ask you to come to the station for an interview."

"You're arresting me?"

"Not at this moment, no," Carrie said, "but I am prepared to, failing your voluntary cooperation."

The principal looked Carrie up and down. Carrie's jacket was slightly open and her badge and holstered Glock partially visible. Seeing it, the high school principal accepted for the first time that she was confronted by the law and that the officer was not going to accept being challenged. Something inside her, a spark of defiant authority, finally caved, and she surrendered. Anything was better than the total humiliation of being seen escorted to a police car by a cop. It was lunchtime and the yard was filled with those students who had preferred to bring their own and were eating and hanging out. Within two hours, Facebook would be enlivened with their delighted reports.

Five minutes later, Carrie, after politely thanking Frances Aster for her civic-minded cooperation, was making her way through the crowd of teenaged kids and getting into her unmarked police car. She felt relieved. She had what was needed and sooner than she expected. What she faced now was hours of bit-by-bit exhaustive interviews with reluctant or openly lying children, their parents with them for the most part hostile in their defensiveness.

The thought was daunting, and something in Carrie balked. It was the kind of detective work she found inexpressively boring. She decided to delay. Irene didn't have to know that she'd wrapped up her interview with the high school principal in less than fifteen minutes. She'd find a way to kill time. Perhaps a good idea would be not to wait until tomorrow but to visit Terry's Old Mill now, size it up herself, and his chances at converting it to condos and a shopping mall. It would fit with her deciding not to let her job as a cop completely take over her life, and something to talk about at bedtime.

She punched in his phone number. "Hi, it's me," and when he'd replied, wondering why she'd called midday, she said, "I'm free for an hour or so. Thought I'd look over your Old Mill project with you. Can you break free?"

Disappointingly, it turned out he couldn't. "Sorry, love—have to attend a conference with the mayor. But hell, go over there yourself, have a look around. And be careful if you go inside. Stay away from the machinery, and watch out for holes in the floor."

Not far away, and as Carrie pulled away from the police station on her way to the Old Mill in the far suburbs, Irene Chagas was returning from a successful interview with the owner of a shop that sold video cameras as well as every sort of computer and cell phone equipment. At the top of her notebook were the three names of those students who in the previous week had bought video tape.

She happened to look up as Carrie drove by, recognizing the unmarked police car, and half unconsciously, at the same time also noticed the out-of-state license plate on the pickup truck that pulled out after Carrie and seemed to stay on Carrie's tail.

Something rang a bell. Hadn't she seen the same pickup truck drive away from near the police station an hour ago when she set out walking to the video camera shop?

Getting back to her desk in the police office and not finding Carrie there, she asked Bruzek, then others where Carrie had gone, and got the same reply, "Thought she went to the high school."

Further thought was cut short by Tom Parrier calling her in to ask about a case she'd worked on, and it was some time before Irene got back to her desk. When she did, she found herself again wondering where Carrie was. Was she being an alarmist? she wondered. Maybe, maybe not. She thought a moment longer: police work required checking everything, even the impossible.

She put in a call to Carrie. No answer. Another try several moments later also got no reply. Now more puzzled than ever, she called the high school and got the same result, with a frosty explanation from Frances Aster, the principal, that some policewoman had come and gone with a list of Michelle Richardson's classmates.

It was part of Irene Chagas's makeup that she carefully stored personal information on virtually every employee with whom she worked. Carrie was no exception. Irene thumbed through a list she kept in a small notebook she always carried, came up with a number for Terry Warner, and punched it in. She got no answer. Perhaps she'd done the wrong number? She checked her notebook punched in the number again. Two rings and it was answered. "Warner. I'm in conference. Will call you back."

"Terry," Chagas said quickly, "Irene Chagas at the station. I'm looking for Carrie. Any idea of where she might be?"

Carrie had told Terry that Irene Chagas was nothing but trouble. He remembered her saying, "And I'm goddamned stuck with her as a boss."

Terry mentally debated how to reply. Maybe it was nothing, he hoped so, and said to Chagas, "She could be off checking out the Old Mill. Sorry, can't talk more." Then, without waiting for her to speak further, he abruptly rang off. If he'd got Carrie in trouble, too bad. He couldn't go through life with her worrying about her job security.

Oh, for Christ's sake, Irene thought. *What the hell is the girl doing? She's supposed to be here at work.*

She thought a moment longer and suddenly stopped being angry: her partner off on her own with a pickup truck apparently following her, and memories of the pickup truck being used to kill Judith Freedman came back in a rush; her examining it at the truck rental parking lot and talking to the boy polishing up cars and trucks, waiting for renters to drive them away.

Irene left her desk, went to the police parking lot downstairs, and slid her tall lanky frame behind the wheel of one of the police cars parked there.

Forty

T HE OLD MILL WAS located in one of those long-abandoned small industrial parks that stain the outskirts of some cities that lack sufficient finance either to raze or develop them. With invading countryside half surrounding the one in which the Old Mill had once been the center of activity, there was a sense of desolation in the heavy clumps of weeds, and even small saplings here and there, that had pushed their way upward through cracks in the unused pavement.

Dominated by the sheer size of the decaying structure, a handful of small brick buildings close by, which had also been constructed more than a century ago, had once housed offices, storage facilities, and minor manufacturing that didn't need power. Carrie drove slowly past them, pulled up outside the Old Mill itself, and got out of the car. Leaning against its front fender, she took a long careful look at what she'd come to see: Terry's plans for which she knew he so badly wanted to share with her.

The Old Mill was a long, rectangularly narrow building. Its worn redbrick exterior, dark with age, was stained with streaks of water runoff that came down through rusted-out gutters from its decaying slate roof. In places it was half-covered by ugly climbing vines.

At first sight, its height made it look as though it had at least three stories, but Carrie quickly realized that was because both its first and second floors had unusually high ceilings, as shown by the two long lines of windows on each, the glass panes of most either broken or dirty with unwashed age.

'Not such a good first impression,' she thought. But envisioning the building scrubbed, the widows replaced with broader bigger ones, perhaps some of its condos with balconies, and imagining a busy ground floor with a large modern entrance to a shopping mall, she began to think that Terry was right in his pursuit.

"Okay," she said aloud to the old building. "Let's take a look at you inside," and she went to an opening that had once supported a double door.

It was a warm day but cloudy, and without any semblance of electric lighting, Carrie found it hard to see once she'd stepped inside. It took a moment for her eyes to adjust, and when they did, she still found it gloomy, with dark shadows everywhere. Beginning to wish she'd chosen a brighter day, she saw she was in one huge room devoted to all sorts of ancient iron machinery. A broad wooden stair nearby, or what was left of one, led upstairs to a half floor above that left the half of the building in which she was standing an open space, right to its high-above iron rafters.

Faintly hearing a rush of water somewhere, she remembered that the Old Mill was by a fast-moving stream known locally as the Narrow River, which rang through the outskirts of Union City. Attracted by the sound, she began to carefully make her way across a wide expanse to the opposite side of the building that was separated almost it's full building length into aisles, cut occasionally by wide traverse spaces crossing from one side of the mill to the other.

Skirting fallen debris and ducking here and there around heavy half-rusted machinery, she reached a large railed-off open space that was occupied by the Mill's enormous paddle wheel. Its wide flat wooden blades supported by a heavy iron frame were, for the most part, partially moss-covered. When put in action it would slowly be turned by the powerful force of river water rushing against each flat blade that would meet it in turn. Several head-height levers that activated the giant wheel stood silently on a steel platform just to one side of the barrier.

Oh, of course, Carrie thought. *they used the river's waterpower to provide electricity and also make their machinery run.* And, looking more closely, she saw that the wheel was indeed connected to a heavy set of gears that in turn, she decided, had once been used to activate overhead leather belts leading to various machinery. Probably to lathes of one kind or another, she thought. Or machinery for cutting or bending metal.

She glanced at the expensive wristwatch Terry had given her as a birthday present. It was well past the lunch hour. Time for her to go, if for no reason other than to avoid some caustic remark from her partner, who would want to know why her interview with the school principal had taken so long.

She slowly made her way back across the Old Mill and had just got to the door when she noticed the pickup truck parked by her police car outside. *Oh, dear,* she thought. *Has to be a caretaker, who will want to know what I'm doing in here.*

The thought had only just formed when she was seized from behind in a grip of iron that pinned her arms to her side and almost stopped her breath. Simultaneously a wide strip of duct tape was slapped across her mouth, stifling her scream. A heavy blow stopped her kicking and any further struggling. Her arms were roughly yanked behind her back and her wrists taped together. Then the same was done to her ankles. And through a blur in her dizziness, she felt her Glock handgun yanked from its holster strapped at her waist and barely saw to when it was it shoved into the waistband of a shorth balding man in a business suit just as he said, "Get her feet."

Almost immediately, then, she felt herself being dragged across the mill's rubble-strewn floor. Her head scraped and slamming into chunks of debris concrete and metal until she came up hard against the rail protecting the big paddle wheel and saw the second man, taller and gray-haired and also in a business suit.

For the first time, true terror gripped her. Everything around her became clear: the mill, the men. Two men had been the murderers of Judith Freedman and of Janet and Sidney Weiss.

One of them, the short balding one, bent low

over her, his face close to hers. "Like fresh water? Yes? Well, you're going for a brief swim, and then I think you will fill us in on any new evidence you have."

There was a sudden sharp sheet of pain across her face that felt like it was on fire. The man waved the duct tape he'd ripped off. "Don't want this if you need a drink, too, do you?"

He was smiling. She wanted to spit in his face and couldn't. Her knees jerked up and she kicked hard. He let out a shout and reared back.

The older man laughed. "Okay, let's do it."

He seized her feet again he said, "Water boarding time." The balding man grabbed at her neck and hair. She was pulled through the gap in the railing and onto one of the big motionless blades of the paddle wheel. She heard the rip of duct tape and felt it run around her waist, fastening her hard to its surface. Just able to turn her head, she saw both men now back behind the rail, only a few feet away. The short balding one seized one of the big levers, slowly moving it.

The big paddle wheel began to move very slowly. The blade she was on began tipping forward, and her with it, her feet first into the river, and as it gathered speed, her legs and her body following, then her head.

There was the rushing sound of the river that became a roar as she went into it. Without thinking she drew in breath at the last second. Water pummeled and beat at her. She wanted to breathe and didn't. She wanted to scream and couldn't, and struggled, and knew she would drown. The need to breathe became worse and worse until she couldn't hold her breath any longer. It felt the first agony of drowning. Her thinking stopped. Everything became dark.

Forty-One

SHE SLOWLY CAME OUT of the water, feet first, gasping, vomiting. The great wheel stopped. She was unstrapped, yanked off it through the railing and back onto the Mill floor. Dimly, she saw again a face bent over her. This time it was the older man who jabbed her repeatedly with a thick finger. "Enjoy your swim?" He laughed. "Care for another, or do you want to talk instead, tell us everything?"

Talk; tell the man anything. She tried to speak. Couldn't.

The balding man reappeared. "Okay. Last chance." Again he was close to her, his breath on her face. She was to remember the smell of it—coffee. And something else. Apple?

Then suddenly—the deafening shot. The air around her seemed to explode. There was a frantic whirring of pigeons, almost as loud a sound as dozens roosting on the rafters high overhead swirled aimlessly in a fluttering terrified cloud.

A second shot. The balding man bending over her, face close, was yanked away by an invisible hand to lie on his back across her legs, half his head gone, his blood becoming a lake around her feet.

Unthinking, knowing only that he was gone, feeling his weight on her, Carrie struggled and freed herself from his body. And, awkwardly half-sitting, saw someone. Who was it? Gun in hand and not far away, they were coming toward her. It was Irene.

Confusion. The shock of surprise. Irene? What was she doing here? Then Irene's suddenly turning away, shooting again off to one side before ducking out of sight.

Another shot, the third one. Another uproar of pigeons. Silence once more. Only the sound of the pigeons that slowly ebbed away.

Carrie tried to think. Get loose. Now and fast. In the gloom she saw a rusted-out forklift platform close by. She rolled and twisted to it, got her back against one corner so she could feel a half rusted-out branch of its cold metal end between her arms, moved herself up and down against its jagged surface. Hard. Over and over, the metal gouging and ripping her arms. She prayed, "Tear, tear," and finally heard the duct tape rip. More, more. Please God, tear. And it tore again.

She felt her arms free. In a sea of pain, she got them around to the front of her and pulled the blood-soaked duct tape loose from around her ankles. She tried to stand, couldn't, crawled slowly back to the dead balding man. He was face down. Grasping his belt, she rolled his inert heavy body half over, tried not to see his shredded half face, pulled her Glock from his waistband.

It was bloodied and slippery. Her hand, too. She pulled out her shirt from the front of her jeans, half wiped both gun and hands with it, tried to rise. "Get up, Carrie, Get up." Her one wounded leg, the one with the bullet, screamed pain. One hand reached and grasped blindly at a piece of machinery, pulling, helping her up. She stood, clinging to part of a long silent lathe.

She fought being dizzy. Listened for some sound, heard only the river over the pounding of her heart. Where was Irene? Had she really seen her? How did Irene know she was here? Where was the other man? It had to be the tall, older one. She wanted to call out but knew she had to keep silent. Any sound would give her away, bring him on her.

She knew she couldn't stay there. In the half darkness, she saw another machine to cling to, dragged away from the dead man, got to it. Then, very carefully, step by step, she headed for the big open doors, holding fast to machinery, crossing one narrow aisle, then another. Looking, seeing, and hearing no one.

Where was the man? And Irene? Very carefully, she got to a long aisle, wider than the others.

Suddenly, just as she did—another shot.

She froze, holding onto something rusty. Silence again. Only the far-off whisper of the river. Where was he? Where was Irene? She listened, gun ready. Where? Where?

She steadied herself to move forward, then in the half-darkness a shadow moved, and she saw Irene as she suddenly stepped into the aisle from behind machinery and in clear sight. Blood sheeted down from her right shoulder. Her Beretta dangled in her left hand. Irene shouted a warning. "Carrie! Watch your back."

In the same instant, he appeared, the tall older one. He came from between two machines right in front of Carrie, saw Irene and fired, then turned on Carrie, so close to her that she could smell him, and slamming her Glock to one side, swung around his own gun, right in her face.

But he was too late. Another roar of sound as Irene fired again. Once, twice. He fell against Carrie, bringing her down with him, his neck and face both torn away, spattering her with blood and flesh.

Later she wouldn't remember her relief that he was gone. Just continuing fear. She rose, stepping over him, fell, rose, called out, "Irene."

And then saw Irene again. She was down and doubled over. "Irene?" There was no answer. Carrie's own cry again, "Irene? Oh, no. No." She staggered down the aisle to her.

Irene had taken a second shot in the stomach. Her shoulder still poured blood. She was only half conscious. Carrie knelt beside her, fished frantically in Irene's jacket, found her cell. In the half light, she punched a number and said, "Officer down. Officer down. The Old Mill. Ambulance. Urgent."

And said to Irene," I'm here, Irene. I'm here for you. Hang on. Don't die. Don't die." She brushed bloodied hair away from Irene's face, tore off her own jacket, then her shirt, and clamped her shirt onto Irene's shoulder to try to stop the flow of blood.

When police backup arrived, along with the ambulance, and poured into the vast empty Old Mill, they found them like that, Carrie sitting back against some rusted-out machinery, still pressing

her shirt into Irene's shoulder, and Irene unconscious, cradled protectively in Carrie's arms.

Forty-Two

SOMERSVILLE WAS A QUIET place on a summer Sunday. Carrie, who had driven up from Union City to spend the day with her father, was at his kitchen table with him and with police chief Sam Ellis, all three enjoying the hamburgers and fries Carrie had picked up at the Lunch Pail on the way, along with a six-pack of beer.

"When's your operation, Carrie?" came from Sam Ellis.

"In two weeks."

"Luckier this time," George Driscoll said to his friend. "She upped and dodged."

"And got dunked 'stead of another bullet in the leg," Sam Ellis said, with a light chuckle. He twisted the top off a beer bottle.

"Yeah," Carrie said. She really didn't want to talk about it. Not even with two old veteran cops like her father and Sam. She didn't even want to think about it, not ever, and was grateful when her father got conversation off her and onto Irene. "How's your partner doing?" he asked.

"Like you'd think," Carrie said. "She had her second operation yesterday."

"Putting her torn up insides back together," Sam said." Poor woman. She really got hurt bad.

Miracle what they can do today. Been hit in the gut like that, even twenty years ago, would've been curtains."

"Surprised she got caught," George said. "Ambushed, really. Right, Carrie?"

Rebellion surged in Carrie. "Irene wasn't ambushed, Dad. She deliberately came out of hiding to warn me."

And then was silent. Carrie thought she would never understand Irene suddenly appearing. Why was she there? How had she known to come? And then the deathly quiet cat-and-mouse struggle Irene had waged in the half-darkness to keep the second killer away from her after she had eliminated the balding man.

No one could know what it had to be like, stalking a killer amidst all the rusted-out silent heavy machinery while the killer stalked her. And if she slipped up, that was it. There'd be no second chance.

Dimly Carrie heard Sam Ellis said, "The shoulder hit too. She lost a lot of blood. Sliced an artery, doctors said. The way that damned Old Mill looked to me when I did a follow-up with Tom, wonder she didn't get blasted the moment she stepped in the doorway. Those two guys were pros. And instead of her, them guys both ended up dead."

"They ran into a bigger pro," George said.

The two old men launched into reminiscing on police violence way in the past of their own lives, and Carrie's mind drifted away from them. Their voices became a blur. There'd been huge local press coverage of the whole incident and a windfall for Nate Wolkowski, who saw the circulation of his paper double in a week. More important to Carrie than the immediate promotion to detective she'd received from the police commissioner, acting on Tom Parrier's recommendation, had been the reaction she'd got from Terry, who had used the incident to forge full speed ahead on getting the Old Mill turned into condos. Carrie had waited nearly a week after she'd recovered, and in a certain suspense for him to condemn, as usual, her being in police work, but instead he'd surprised her.

"No, love, I don't think you should quit. I think you should stick with it. Being a cop is you, plain and simple. It's you one hundred percent. For you to quit would be to tear out your spirit and throw it to the four winds."

"But what about you?"

"You mean what about us, don't you? The you and me? I'm doing something I love. You're doing your cop thing. We'll be fine."

Her father had echoed that. "Inspector Driscoll, don't you even think of quitting. Being a cop, no thanks to me, is what and who you are."

"It's more like what Irene is than me," Carrie had said. "And now there's no way she can go on working. She's been told she has to do something else."

"Well, she was due to retire anyway, and at least went out in a blaze of good," her father said. "Tell her to come see me and I'll fix things up for her down at the post office. She saved my daughter's life. No family? She'd soon find family enough out there on the road delivering mail every day 'cept for Sunday."

Carrie paid her usual daily visit to Irene in the hospital the next evening. She'd stopped bringing her flowers. Irene's room had been so filled for days with police floral offerings from every cop from Chief Parrier on down that the nurses had started distributing them throughout the hospital to others. She was a cop's cop, everyone said, and an honor to the oath she took to serve and protect.

Carrie had learned that Irene was crazy for pastry, and instead of flowers always brought her some. Today it was a couple of chocolate éclairs that Irene insisted they share.

They ate the éclairs in silence, until after a while Irene said, "Visit your father? Yes, I think I'd like that." She smiled. "Help him keep an eye on my partner, make sure she toed the line."

After a while, Irene fell asleep, and Carrie quietly left. It was late. Tomorrow was another day, and she was a cop with police work to do.

About the Author

Born to wealth and privilege in New York, David Osborn chose to spurn both as false icons after World War II combat as a Marine Corps dive bomber pilot. On his own and following brief careers in television and public relations, he expatriated to France when falsely accused of un-Americanism in the infamous Senator McCarthy era, paying his way with a co-authored first motion picture script, *Chase a Crooked Shadow*. When its star-studded success took him from laboring in a rock quarry in France into Britain's film industry, he was launched on a long world-class writing career that saw him dangerously engaged during several Cold War years with Czech anticommunist resistance behind the Iron Curtain. Living in France and England as well as isolated for twelve years in a tiny Alpine village in Switzerland, Osborn authored numerous stellar TV plays and a score of major motion pictures, including *The Trap*, which earned an Academy Award nomination. Turning novelist with the critical success of *The Glass Tower* followed by the world best-selling classics *Open Season*, *The French Decision*, *Love and Treason*, and a half dozen more outstanding thrillers, he has had many imitators, but none reaching the startling originality of his stories, the stunning impact of his flawless page-turning plots, and his literate prose in each that packs a powerful punch with nearly every line.

Also by David Osborn

Novels and Screenwriting

Novels

The Glass Tower – Hodder & Stoughton
Open Season – The Dial Press
The French Decision – Doubleday
Love and Treason – New American Library
Heads – Bantam
Murder on Martha's Vineyard – Lynx
Murder on the Chesapeake – Simon & Schuster
Murder in the Napa Valley – Simon & Schuster
The Last Pope – Source Books
The Cape Cod Blue – Dagmar Miura
Alicia's Secret (young adult) – Dagmar Miura
A Cold Wind from the Andes – Dagmar Miura
The Head Hunters – Dagmar Miura
Looking Back: The Long Life of a Writer (a memoir)
Delta Red – Dagmar Miura
Eventide – Dagmar Miura
The Somersville Bodies – Dagmar Miura
Cold Case 369 – Dagmar Miura
The Lighthouse (a novella)– Dagmar Miura
The Saugatuck Conspiracy – Dagmar Miura

For Children

Jessica and the Crocodile Knight (a novel)
– HarperCollins

Jessica and Her Adventures in Fairyland (collection of five novellas) – Dagmar Miura

Ophelia and Her Forest Friends (series of ten stories) – Dagmar Miura

Jessica and the Witch's Broom – Dagmar Miura

Jessica and the Flying Unicorns – Dagmar Miura

Jessica and the Golden Swan Feather – Dagmar Miura

Feature Films

The Trap (original story and screenplay; Academy Award nominee for Best Foreign Film)
– Columbia

Open Season (screenplay, adapted from Osborn's own best-selling novel *Open Season*) – Columbia

Chase a Crooked Shadow (original story and screenplay co-written with Charles Sinclair; listed by the British Academy of Motion Picture Science as "One of the ten best suspense scripts ever written") – Warner Bros.

Moment of Danger, a.k.a. *Malaga* (screenplay adapted from the novel) – Warner Bros.

Malaga (screenplay) – Warner Bros.

Maroc 7 (original story and screenplay) – J. Arthur Rank

Deadlier Than the Male (original story and screenplay) – J. Arthur Rank

Some Girls Do (original story and screenplay) – J. Arthur Rank

The Road to Dusty Death (screenplay) – J. Arthur Rank

The Games (screenplay) – Associated British

Follow the Boys (original story and screenplay)
    – MGM

Beat Girl (original story and screenplay) – Renown
    Films/British Lion

Stop-over Forever (original story and screenplay) –
    British Lion

Winter Holiday (original story and screenplay)
    – MGM

Penny Gold (original story and screenplay) – J.
    Arthur Rank/Columbia

Whoever Slew Auntie Roo? (original story and
    screenplay) – Paramount & American
    International

Murder, She Said (screenplay, Agatha Christie
    adaptation) – MGM

Murder at the Gallop (screenplay, Agatha Christie
    adaptation) – MGM

Feature-Length Documentaries

Fangio, The History of Formula One Racing (original
    screenplay; executive producer) – Volpi
    Productions

Why Ireland – Irish Tourist Bureau

Films Canceled While in Production

HMS Ulysses – Volpi Productions (screenplay
    adaptation of the Alistair MacLean novel about
    protecting North Sea convoys to Russia during
    World War II; production halted when a key
    warship was unavailable)

The Mad Motorists – Volpi Productions (screenplay adaptation from the Allen Andrews novel about the 1907 Peking to Paris race)

Eagle at Sundown – Dragon Films (original screen story about Napoleon's escape from Elba; starring Douglas Fairbanks; in production when canceled)

Les Petits Rats – Disney (original story and screenplay about the Paris Ballet school; production begun, then canceled)

Hunters' Horn – McCahon Productions (screenplay adaptation from the Harriette Simpson Arnow novel; production canceled; financing failure)

Blood on the Rose – British Lion (screenplay adaptation from the Phyllis Hastings novel)

Television

Bouquet for Miss Olive (three-act play; British Television Producers Association nominee for Best Play of the Year) – Granada/ITV

Three on a Gas Ring (three-act play; British Television Producers Association nominee for Best Play of the Year) – Granada/ITV

Why George Brown Hanged (three-act play) – Granada/ITV

Arthur of the Britons (pilot and three scripts on the life of King Arthur; Writers Guild of Great Britain award winner for Best British Children's Series)

The Antiquers (original story, pilot, and six episodes in the sitcom series) – Irish National Television